DRAGON

DRAGON AMERICA

MIKE RESNICK

A PHOBOS IMPACT BOOK
AN IMPRINT OF PHOBOS BOOKS
NEW YORK

PHOBOS
IMPACT

A Phobos Impact Book
Published by Phobos Books
200 Park Avenue South
New York, NY 10003
www.phobosweb.com

Distributed in the United States by National Book Network, Lanham, Maryland.

Cover by Zuccadesign

Library of Congress Cataloging-in-Publication Data

Resnick, Michael D.
　　Dragon America / Mike Resnick.
　　　p. cm.
　　ISBN 0-9720026-9-3 (pbk. : alk. paper)
　　1. United States—History—Revolution, 1775–1783—Fiction.
　2. Washington, George, 1732–1799—Fiction. 3. Boone, Daniel, 1734–1820—Fiction. 4. Dragons—Fiction. I. Title.
　PS3568.E698D73 2005
　813'.54—dc22

　　　　　　　　　　　　　　　　　　　　　　　　　　　　　　2005011282

∞™ The paper used in this publication meets the minimum requirements of American National Standard for Information Sciences—Permanence of Paper for Printed Library Materials, ANSI/NISO Z39.48-1992

To Carol, as always

And to John Ordover

CONTENTS

HISTORICAL NOTE

In the summer of 2005 A.D., more than half a millennium
after Christopher Columbus reached the New World, a
science fiction writer named Robert A. Heinlein wrote a
rigorously extrapolated novel entitled *Mammal America*,
which hypothesized that when the Europeans first set
foot on the North American continent, they found themselves surrounded by the same mammalian ecology that
existed throughout Europe, Asia, and Africa.

In *Mammal America*, Heinlein reinstalled the long-
vanished land bridge to Russia by the simple expedient
of moving the cataclysmic eruption that occurred in the
Bering Strait to the distant island of Java. He further suggested that the runaway asteroid that crashed down just
south of Mexico a few million years ago was small
enough to burn up in the Earth's atmosphere—which is
to say, he proposed yet another land bridge, this one
known as Central America, which attached us to South
America.

Thus, in Heinlein's imagined future, the North American continent was not cut off from the rest of the world, and mammals, rather than dragons, filled most of the major ecological niches.

The book became an international bestseller, and quickly inspired four nonfiction books explaining why Heinlein, who never claimed to be writing anything but fiction, was mistaken in his assumptions, and why it was far more likely that America's dragons would have crossed the Bering Strait and populated Russia and then the entire Asian and European continents if a land bridge had existed.

Soon still more books on the subject appeared, video "documentaries" of an America populated by Heinlein's mammals were created using the latest CGI technology and proved wildly popular, mammal and dragon experts were scheduled opposite each other on all the talk shows, and more than one fistfight broke out between otherwise sedate scholars.

"Now I know how Dan Brown feels," remarked Heinlein, referring to the author of *The Michelangelo Code*, another work of fiction that had elicited the same type of misguided academic response a few years earlier.

Fortunately for all of us, *Mammal America* really was just what Heinlein claimed it was: a work of speculative fiction. It *is* fascinating, however, to consider how history might have turned out had even some of his fanciful speculations been correct.

DRAGON AMERICA

PART ONE

DANIEL BOONE'S BOOK

CHAPTER ONE

A lone figure stalked the hills and valleys that would someday become Cincinnati, rifle in hand, careful to tread softly. A small greenish creature perched on his shoulder, as alert as he himself was.

"Hush!" whispered the man.

He bent over and examined the ground with his trained eye. Here was a broken twig, there was a shrub with a few leaves rubbed off—not eaten, because they lay on the ground, but rubbed. He walked a few steps farther. There were hundreds of ants scurrying around. They weren't foraging for food. In fact, they seemed purposeless, which implied that they had no purpose, and that in turn implied that his prey had stepped on their mound and destroyed it. And recently. Ants didn't remain without purpose for long. In another few minutes they'd be rebuilding their home if it was salvageable, or creating a new one if it wasn't.

Then he came to the surest sign of all that he was on the right trail: a small pile of pellet-shaped dung. He knelt down and inserted a finger into it. Still almost body-temperature. He was close.

Suddenly the green creature emitted a hissing shriek, leaped off his shoulder, flew forward a dozen feet, grabbed a dragonfly in midair, crunched it between powerful jaws, and then flew leisurely back to the man's shoulder.

"If you've frightened away my dinner, I just may take a bite out of you," murmured the man.

The sound of a dragon's screech came to his ears.

"Well, you attracted *someone's* attention," said the man. "I just wish I knew if it was a dragon or a Shawnee."

A second scream.

The creature tensed, then flew off into the woods.

The man breathed a sigh of relief. He couldn't differentiate between a dragon's scream and a Shawnee signaling to his fellow warriors by emulating a dragon's scream, but his little pet could. It would be back in a few minutes, torn and bleeding if the scream had come from a territorial male, and looking exceptionally pleased with itself if it had come from a female.

In the meantime, he would continue the hunt. He hadn't eaten in close to two days. Initially he'd filled his stomach with wild berries and the edible bark of some trees, but he knew he would need all his strength now that he was preparing to cross the broad Ohio River and enter the heart of Shawnee country. He didn't like announcing his presence with the blast of his rifle, but it was going to be known sooner or later. After all, he was here to parley with Blackfish, not avoid him. He just wanted to get close enough so that when he finally ran into a party of Shawnee they wouldn't decide that they were too far away to bother taking him to Blackfish and try to kill him instead.

It was a possibility. There was always a chance that the first Shawnee he encountered would not know that Daniel Boone was the adopted son of the great Blackfish.

And even if they did know, there was nothing to stop them from killing him and burying him in a shallow grave deep in the woods, where no one would ever know that he'd even been in the territory. The only reason Blackfish had made him his son was that he feared massive reprisals if he killed the famous Daniel Boone. It hadn't, Boone noted bitterly, stopped him from killing numerous settlers who had accompanied Boone on his several trips to Kentucky. More than once Boone was the only survivor, and only because Blackfish had decreed that no one could kill his adopted son.

There was a sudden hint of motion off to his left, and Boone froze. Whatever had moved froze as well. Boone peered at the spot, squinting his eyes, looking away, then looking back—and, as had happened so often in the past, what was initially hidden from him was suddenly visible. It was a female Fleetrunner, slim and sleek. He'd known that it was female because it hadn't been marking its territory as he stalked it, and the branches that a taller male would have broken off were untouched. She stood motionless, not looking at him, instinctively aware that the sun could glint off her eye if she faced him.

He slowly raised his rifle to his shoulder. It had been loaded since he'd picked up her trail, so at least he wouldn't have to load it while hoping that she remained where she was. He took aim, a few inches behind her left shoulder. He wanted to aim a little lower, for the dragon's heart was lower than that of most mammals, but there was a branch in the way. He carefully squeezed the trigger, the forest reverberated to the sound of the shot, birds and small flying dragons began screaming, and an instant later the dragon was not there.

At first he thought she might have fallen where she stood, but nothing short of a brain shot would accomplish that. They had remarkable vitality, these Ohio dragons. He ran over to where she'd been when he shot her, and found traces of foamy blood, which meant his bullet had pierced one or both lungs. Though he couldn't see her he knew she was running right this second . . . but he also knew that she couldn't run for long. It was just a matter of following the blood spoor until he came to a dead or dying Fleetrunner lying on the ground.

He heard a fluttering behind him and turned to see the little dragon approaching him.

"Hello, Banshee," he said. "I hope you enjoyed yourself."

He had a feeling that if dragons could speak, he would be regaled with an all-too-vivid account of the last five minutes.

Boone held an arm out, and as if on command, the little dragon walked down it toward his wrist. Then the man picked it up with both hands and held it next to the foamy blood.

"Take a good sniff of it," said Boone. "All right," he continued, tossing the dragon into the air. "Go find it."

Banshee flew off, gaining height with each beat of its iridescent, scaly wings. When the dragon was perhaps seventy feet high, it began making larger and larger circles, looking for all the world like a raptor riding the warm thermals and searching for prey.

Finally Banshee screamed and plunged toward the ground a mile away. Boone set off in that direction. When he'd covered about three-quarters of the distance, Banshee flew up to him and hovered in front of him.

"Did you find her?"

The little dragon hissed softly.

"Well, get on my shoulder and we'll go find her."

The dragon continued to hover.

"What's the matter with you?" said Boone, moving to his left to step around the dragon.

Banshee moved to remain in front of him, blocking his way.

"Look," said Boone irritably, "if you want to visit your ladyfriend again, be my guest—but get out of my way. I'm hungry."

He reached out and grabbed the little dragon. Banshee flapped its wings furiously and began hissing, but when it couldn't break free of Boone's grasp it finally relaxed, and Boone placed it on a shoulder. It hissed and shrieked, but remained where it was.

"I think it's this way," said Boone, heading off. He spotted some foamy bright red blood on the trunk of a small maple tree. "Right. This way."

He kept walking while Banshee's shrieks and screams became louder and more urgent. Finally he stepped into a clearing and found just what was frightening his pet.

The Fleetrunner was dead, stretched out on the ground—but she wasn't alone.

A trio of Nightkillers—blue-green dragons with broad black stripes, each perhaps 150 pounds—had encircled the corpse and were tearing pieces of meat from it. One of them looked up at Boone, who was some fifty feet away, and uttered a short, ominous hiss while simultaneously displaying a mouthful of razor-sharp fangs.

Boone raised his rifle, only to realize that he hadn't reloaded it. Besides, it wouldn't do much good. Shoot one Nightkiller and the other two would tear him to shreds before he could fire a second shot.

He looked around for the rest of the pack. Nightkillers usually traveled in groups of up to a dozen. To see only three on a kill was rare—and even as the thought crossed his mind, two more Nightkillers emerged from the forest and hopped across to the Fleetrunner's corpse.

Boone hated to give up the Fleetrunner that he'd gone to the trouble to stalk and kill, but he knew he was over-matched by the blue-green dragons, and so he slowly backed away. Once they were out of sight, Banshee's courage returned and it hissed fiercely in the direction of the Nightkillers.

"I admire your bravery," muttered Boone.

He'd had the little pet for almost five years now. One morning he woke up and there it was, sitting a few feet away and staring at him. He'd offered it enough different tidbits to learn that Darters—Banshee's species—were strictly insectivores. But it seemed to appreciate the fact that he was trying to feed it, and after a while it hopped up on his shoulder. From that moment to this it had rarely been out of his presence, and it had proven useful on more than one occasion, as it had this afternoon. It could spot enemies and wounded animals from high overhead, though it had no way of communicating ex-actly *what* it had spotted. He thought Banshee felt a bond with him, but it was always possible that the little dragon was staying around simply through force of habit. There was a lot that even he didn't know about dragons—and *that* was going to be a serious problem on his mission.

There weren't a lot of nuts or berries around, but he found enough to assuage his hunger and topped them off by beating Banshee to a couple of grasshoppers. The dragon's face was relatively devoid of expression, but its entire demeanor implied that its best friend had just be-trayed it.

They reached the river just before nightfall. It was a full mile wide at this point. Boone had no intention of swimming it, and he didn't feel like building a canoe that he wouldn't need again for months or even longer. He found a fallen tree, hacked off a five-foot section of its trunk, took a branch as a paddle, then carried it to the river. He dragged it into the water, sat astride it, and using the branch as a rudder slowly made his way across the river. The current carried him six miles downstream before he made it to the Kentucky side, but that was of no concern to him. Blackfish never stayed in one place for very long; he was as likely to find him six miles downstream as six, or ten, or thirty, miles upstream.

He climbed off the log in waist-deep water and let it float away. Banshee had no aversion to bathing in every lake or river they came to, but hated to be splashed, and took off from Boone's shoulder when they were still fifty yards from shore. As soon as the man clambered onto the bank, the little Darter was back on his shoulder, hissing and screeching as if to voice its displeasure about their recent means of transportation.

Boone paid no attention to the dragon. As soon as he himself was dry he went to work on his rifle, cleaning and wiping it, and then made sure that his powder horn hadn't been damaged by the river, and that the powder within it had remained dry.

It would be dark in another hour, so there was no sense traveling any farther. Instead he built himself a small lean-to from fallen branches, then gathered some kindling and lit a fire. Banshee, as usual, paid no attention to it. Boone knew that some varieties of dragon could, on occasion, produce a flame that would shoot forth from their mouths, but he'd never seen a Darter do it. It was a pity, he reflected; it could have saved him a lot of effort every time he had to start a fire.

Somewhere in the middle of the night he was awakened as Banshee cuddled next to him for warmth. He tossed two more logs on the dying fire, and that kept the chill off the air until morning.

When he got up Banshee was already busy gobbling up every insect in the area. He slung his pack over one shoulder, his rifle over the other, and began walking. He had no idea where he was going, because he had no idea where Blackfish was, but he knew if he made enough noise—and Boone, who could be as silent as a shadow, made sure he made noise—sooner or later he'd come to the Shawnee's attention.

As it turned out, it was sooner. Less than an hour after he started walking, he found himself confronting two Shawnee, who suddenly appeared about eighty feet ahead of him. He didn't have to look to know that there'd be at least one on each side of him and one behind him.

"It took you long enough," he said in their language.

"You will come with us, Sheltowee," said one of the warriors, using his Shawnee name.

"You will take me to Blackfish?" asked Boone.

"Yes."

"Then let's go."

"You were ordered never to return to our land," said the warrior, as they began walking.

"I miss my father," said Boone.

"It was your father who told you never to return."

"He was having a bad morning," said Boone. "I'm sure he misses me as much as I miss him."

"We shall see." The warrior paused. "Why do you carry that dragon on your shoulder?"

"Because he's too small to carry me."

"I have heard about Sheltowee's sense of humor," said the warrior. Then: "What a shame that I have never seen any evidence of it."

"You are cruel, my brother," said Boone. "But since I will be spending time with the Shawnee, I forgive you."

"I did not ask your forgiveness."

"Then it is the more freely given."

The warrior stared coldly at him. "Where are your friends and relatives, Sheltowee? Always you come to our land with many people, and always Blackfish kills them or chases them away."

"Think of the time and energy I saved them by telling them to stay home this time," said Boone.

A look of contempt spread across the warrior's face. "What can one expect of a turtle?"

"A *big* turtle," Boone corrected him, for the literal translation of "*Sheltowee*" was "Big Turtle."

"Enough," said the warrior. "If you speak again I will kill your pet."

"If you do I will kill you," said Boone coldly.

"All of us?" asked the warrior, amused.

"All of you."

"And if we kill you first?"

"Then you will have to explain to Blackfish why you killed his adopted son," said Boone.

The warrior considered that statement, and decided to walk in stoic silence.

Too bad, thought Boone as they trudged through the undergrowth. *If Blackfish knew what I have come all this way to talk him into, he might very well reward you for killing me now.*

CHAPTER TWO

It took a full day and a night to reach Blackfish, for the Shawnee's territory was not small. Along the way one of the warriors killed a deer with a bow and arrow, and begrudgingly allowed Boone to partake of the meat after the Shawnee had taken what they wanted. At night Boone tied a rope around Banshee's neck and tied the other end to his wrist. The little dragon wasn't happy about it, but Boone knew that if Banshee wandered too near the Shawnee while he was sleeping they would probably kill him. The Shawnee had no use for dragons, except for big beasts of burden they called Landwagons.

It was at noon on the next day that they reached Blackfish's camp. The chief's lodge was quite elegant for an Indian dwelling, and his eldest wife was the first to see Boone approaching. She immediately stood up and began hurling curses at him.

"I'm glad to see you too, Mother," said Boone.

Soon the entire village was lining the path, staring at Boone and his little dragon as they walked the last fifty yards. Some seemed merely curious; others looked like they wanted nothing more than to see the notorious Sheltowee dead after a sufficiently long period of suffering.

Finally Blackfish emerged from his lodge, tall, dignified, gray-haired, carrying half a hundred battle scars, a little heavier than the last time Boone had seen him, but every inch a ruler of men.

Boone stopped a few feet from him.

"Greetings, my father," he said.

"Where are your companions?" demanded Blackfish.

"I've come alone this time," replied Boone. "Except for my pet," he added, indicating Banshee, who perched on his left shoulder.

"You have great tenacity," said Blackfish. "I keep banishing you from my land, and you keep coming back. Am I going to have to incarcerate you again, Sheltowee?"

Boone shook his head. "I come as your son."

Blackfish sighed. "You always come as my son. And you always bring people with you who try to steal my land."

"Look around me," said Boone. "Talk to your scouts. I have brought no one."

"What do you want, Sheltowee?"

"We must talk."

"We *are* talking."

"Alone."

Blackfish smiled. "So that you can kill me? I know your skills, Sheltowee. I will not place myself in your power, for in battle you have no more mercy than I myself have."

"I'm here to talk, not to fight."

"I will have six warriors present," said Blackfish. "Otherwise, your visit is at an end, and you must leave my land before nightfall or I will keep you captive for three months, as I did when I first adopted you."

Boone considered the Shawnee's counteroffer, and nodded his agreement. "All right. Six warriors."

"We will begin in two hours."

"Why not now?" asked Boone.

"I must send for the man Girty. It will take one hour to reach him, and one hour for him to arrive."

"Is he still with you?"

"You object?"

"Of course I object," said Boone. "Simon Girty is an evil man. He sold information to America's enemies, and is even now in the employ of the British."

"He speaks very highly of them."

"He would," snorted Boone. "They pay him enough."

"Must I remind you, Sheltowee, that the British have never bothered the Shawnee, whereas you alone have killed some fifty of my warriors."

"They attacked me."

"You tried to steal our land."

"We can share the land and live in peace," said Boone.

"We can live in peace," responded Blackfish. "You in your Carolina, and we in the land that has always belonged to the Shawnee."

"I didn't come here to argue with you," said Boone. "Let us go inside your lodge and talk."

Blackfish summoned two young warriors, spoke softly to them, and watched them leave at a trot. "They have gone to get Simon Girty."

"If you wish to talk while we are waiting for him, I will summon one who speaks your own language."

"You have another American living here?" asked Boone, surprised.

"He is not one of the Long Knives," answered Blackfish. He turned to another warrior. "Bring Pompey."

The warrior left, and returned a moment later with a tall black man, dressed in buckskins, with a hatchet tucked into his belt.

"You sent for me, my chief?" said the man in perfect Shawnee.

"I will be busy for the next two hours," said Blackfish. "It will be your duty to keep my son amused."

The black man frowned. "Which of your sons, my chief?"

"My adopted son," said Blackfish, indicating Boone. He turned and vanished into his lodge.

The black man studied Boone for a long moment. "So you are the legendary Daniel Boone," he said in perfect English.

Boone nodded. "And you are . . . ?"

"My name is Pompey."

"You're no Indian," said Boone. "How did you wind up with the Shawnee?"

"You're no Indian either," replied Pompey with a smile. "How did you wind up as Blackfish's son?"

"I asked you first."

"All right," said Pompey. "We shall go sit in the shade and tell each other our life stories, with minimal embellishment."

Boone looked at the warriors. "Will they let us?"

"Why not? As long as you don't try to run away, I don't see why you can't be comfortable—though how you can be comfortable with a Darter on your shoulder is beyond my reckoning."

"Perhaps because he's the only creature in the village that doesn't want me dead."

"I don't want you dead," said Pompey. "And if Blackfish wanted you dead, we'd be disposing of the corpse right now. Come on."

Pompey walked to a tree with low-hanging branches and sat down with his back against the trunk. Boone followed suit and sat, cross-legged, a few feet from him. Four warriors, spears in hand, immediately walked over and stood just behind him.

"Pay no attention to them," said Pompey. "They can't understand us as long as we speak English—or would you prefer French?"

"English is fine." Pompey nodded.

"Now suppose you tell me who you are and what you're doing living with the Shawnee?" said Boone.

"You already know my name."

"Is Pompey a first or last name?"

"Whichever you prefer" was the reply. "What it isn't is a Christian name. My god remains in Africa, awaiting the return of those members of my tribe who were stolen from our homeland."

"So you're a slave."

Pompey grinned again. "Do I look like a slave?"

"Explain," said Boone impatiently.

"Some people have a knack for singing. Others, like yourself, have a knack for exploring and for fighting. Some, they say, are exceptionally skilled as lovers. But me, I have a special talent: I can pick up almost any language and speak it like a native in a very short time. I speak the Ashanti dialect of my mother, and while I was a child on a plantation in Virginia I learned not only English, but also the languages of the Ibo and Tswana tribes. When my master took a French mistress I learned French just as easily." He paused, as if remembering each new language. "When I was a young man my master sold me to Nathaniel Burke, a trapper who had been unable to learn any of the Indian languages and bought me to act as his interpreter. As it happened, the Shawnee

killed him before I'd learned their language, and took me
prisoner. Once I learned to speak Shawnee, Blackfish
gave me my freedom and asked me to act as his translator in dealings with the white man and other tribes—and
here I am."

"You don't look that young to me."

"I'm thirty." A pause. "Probably," he added.

"How long have you been with the Shawnee?"

"Eleven years."

Boone frowned. "How come I never saw you before?"

"You speak Shawnee, so Blackfish didn't need me.
And he's always afraid I'll run away or that someone
will steal me away, so he doesn't like me to meet with
outsiders except when he's present. There is not an abun-
dance of translators out here."

"You speak very well for a self-taught man," said
Boone.

"My original master encouraged me to learn," said
Pompey. "I can both read and write. Can you?"

"Yes."

"We're probably the only two men for hundreds of
miles who can make that claim," said Pompey.

"There's another," said Boone. "We're waiting for
him."

"Ah," said Pompey. "Simon Girty."

"You know him?"

"Of course. We both live with the Shawnee."

"Someday I'll kill him," said Boone.

"Why?"

"He has betrayed his own country and helped the
British." Pompey looked unimpressed, and Boone
added: "News may not have reached this far inland, but
we're at war with the British."

"You *are* the British," said Pompey.

"No," said Boone. "We are Americans."

"No," said Pompey adamantly. "You are British who live in America."

"Even if you're technically right, it won't be true for long," replied Boone. "We are currently engaged in a war of independence."

"A bunch of farmers and merchants are fighting the British army? I always knew white men were foolish, but until now I didn't think they were suicidal."

"Freedom is a concept worth fighting for," said Boone firmly.

"Not only do I agree with you," said Pompey, "but I think my belief in it predates your own."

"That's why you should sympathize with the Americans."

"The British don't keep slaves. The same can't be said for the Americans. Though to be truthful, my sympathies lie with my own people."

Boone shrugged. "I suppose if I were in your place, I'd feel the same way."

"You're an honest man, Daniel Boone," said Pompey. "I think we're going to become friends."

"I can use all the friends I can get in Blackfish's domain," said Boone sincerely.

"Why are you *in* his domain?"

"Not everyone can afford a plantation or slaves," said Boone. "Most of us can't even afford a patch of land with a house and barn on it. So over the years I've led a number of pilgrimages to the Kentucky side of the Ohio River. We always came in peace, but Blackfish seems to think God gave him all the land south of the river and most of the land leading up to it on the Ohio side. He killed the first group that came with me, and imprisoned me for three months."

"Why didn't he kill you too?" asked Pompey.

"The respect of one warrior for another. I was allowed to go out hunting for meat, but only when his warriors accompanied me. One day I escaped, and walked all the way back to South Carolina on a broken ankle."

"You should have stayed there."

"South Carolina was no more hospitable on my return," answered Boone. "The people were still hungry for land, and the land was still too expensive, so I put together another caravan. This time we knew what to expect, so we built a fort that still exists."

"I've heard of it: Boonesborough."

"I didn't choose the name," said Boone. "Anyway, the Shawnee kept attacking us. We gave as good as we got, but there are a lot more Shawnee than there were settlers." He sighed deeply. "It's been going on for a few years. They're under orders to kill the other white men, but only to capture me."

"Why can't they kill you too?" asked Pompey.

"It wouldn't do for Blackfish to kill even an adopted son," explained Boone. "It might give his own sons ideas about what happens to potential successors who don't take matters into their own hands."

"Then I still don't understand: Why are you here rather than with your own people, defending Boonesborough?"

"That's what I have to talk to Blackfish about."

Suddenly Banshee screeched and flew off, returning a few seconds later chomping happily on the remains of a butterfly.

"I have never seen an Indian domesticate a Darter," observed Pompey. "Why have you done so?"

"I like the company."

"And perhaps he warns you of approaching danger?" suggested Pompey.

"Perhaps," agreed Boone.

"Some of the Landwagons around here are incredibly stubborn," noted Pompey, referring to the beasts of burden. "I'm surprised Blackfish hasn't asked you to help train them."

"All Blackfish ever asks me to do is go back to Carolina and never set foot on his land again."

"Look at it from his point of view," said Pompey. "You *have* already killed a few dozen of his finest warriors."

"I have never fired the first shot or struck the first blow," replied Boone. "If he would let us live in peace, there would be no more violence."

"It's not his nature to live in peace—and from all I hear about the great Daniel Boone, it's not your nature either. If it was, you'd stop trying to settle your people on Shawnee land."

"God didn't give it to them," said Boone. "What makes it theirs?"

"They're willing to fight you for it," answered an amused Pompey. "Isn't that what you're willing to do to keep the British off what you are certain is your land?"

"Are you *sure* we're going to be friends?" said Boone sardonically.

Pompey smiled, walked off for a moment, then returned with a small gourd. "We'll seal our friendship with a drink."

"What is it?" asked Boone.

"Mostly fermented apples that have been mashed to a pulp and then mixed with various juices."

Boone grinned. "I used to make this stuff myself." He accepted the gourd and took a swallow, then made a face. "That's stronger than anything *I* ever made."

"You disapprove?"

"On the contrary. If I could sit down with Blackfish over a couple of gourds of this, we'd be as close as a real father and son by the end of it." He took another swallow. "You speak all those languages, you argue like one of those men in the Continental Congress, and you make

the best drinkin' stuff I've had in years. You have quali-
ties, Pompey. I think you're right: we're going to become
friends."

"Good," said Pompey. "And as an act of friendship,
why don't you tell me some of the experiences that have
made you so famous that even a teenaged slave in Virginia had heard of you half a lifetime ago?"

"I hate to do it," said Boone reluctantly. "It seems like
bragging."

"We're the only ones who speak English, at least until
Simon Girty gets here," said Pompey in a conspiratorial
whisper. "I won't tell anyone if you don't."

For the next ninety minutes Boone related some of his
experiences to Pompey as the two sat beneath the maple
tree, surrounded by Blackfish's warriors. He told of his
excursions into Florida, his trips to what was to become
Tennessee, the death of his oldest son James at the hands
of Indians, the capture of his daughter Jemima by the
Shawnee and his subsequent rescue of her and two of her
friends, his many encounters with Blackfish and his curious relationship with the old chief.

Pompey was still asking Boone questions about his exploits when a burly man with a thick black beard arrived.
He glared at Boone without saying a word, then stalked
past him toward the entrance to Blackfish's lodge. Two
warriors immediately barred his way.

"But he sent for me, damn it!" complained the man in
thickly accented Shawnee.

"No one enters without Blackfish's permission," answered a warrior. "He knows you are here."

The bearded man walked over to where Boone and
Pompey were sitting.

"This has got something to do with you, doesn't it?" he
demanded angrily.

"So now you're talking to Americans, Mr. Girty?" said Boone sarcastically.

"The only Americans I see here all have red skins," answered Girty. "You two are just an Englishman and a slave."

Pompey looked at Boone. "Do you want to kill him, or should I?"

Girty pulled an ax and a hunting knife from his belt, holding one in each hand. "Just try it," he growled. "I'll chop both your heads off and stick them on poles for everyone to see!"

"I will decide who lives and dies on Shawnee land," said a stern voice from behind them. They all turned and found themselves facing Blackfish. "Come into my lodge," he continued. "It is time to find out why Sheltowee has disobeyed his father once again."

CHAPTER THREE

Blackfish seated himself on a small stool. Boone, Girty, and Pompey all sat cross-legged on the floor, so that none of their heads would be higher than his. Six warriors positioned themselves in a circle around the four principals.

"You have come once again to a land that is forbidden to you, Sheltowee," said the chief sternly. "You insist you have come only to talk. But Sheltowee's reputation is almost as great as Blackfish's himself, and his reputation is not as a talker. Therefore, I have summoned Pompey, who knows all languages, to tell me if your words hide other meanings, and Simon Girty, who will inform me if whatever you propose will accrue to the benefit of the Long Knives and the detriment of the Shawnee. Now you may speak."

"Thank you, my father," said Boone. "You are not only the chief of the Shawnee nation, but also the war chief of all the Shawnee. I bring you a message from the war chief of all the Long Knives, proposing an alliance."

"He lies!" snapped Girty. "He's been a settler and an explorer for half his lifetime! Why would he even know the white man's war chief?"

"Do you know his name?" asked Boone mildly.

"Of course I do! It's that traitor to the king, George Washington."

Boone turned to Blackfish. "It is from that very same George Washington that I bring my message."

He reached into a pocket and withdrew a well-worn envelope, which he handed to Pompey.

"As you can see," he said, "it is addressed to me at my farm in South Carolina, and was hand-delivered to me by Edward Rutledge, one of the signers of the Declaration of Independence. It is on General Washington's own stationery, which was a gift to him from Benjamin Franklin."

Boone had no idea who had printed the stationery, and the letter had come to him via his normal once-a-week mail delivery, but he felt that if he mentioned enough names Blackfish might have heard of one of them, which might impress Girty enough to keep him quiet.

"You came from north of the river," noted Blackfish. "That is not the route to Carolina."

"I had to give a wide berth to the British army," explained Boone. "They are ensconced in the South, so I circled around them and came through Pennsylvania and Ohio."

"I see a piece of paper with markings on it," said Blackfish, who clearly had no further interest in Boone's choice of routes. "But I see no purpose in it. I listen, but your General Washington's voice does not come from the paper."

"But it will," answered Boone. "Have you ever given an order that was not carried out, not because you were purposely disobeyed, but because by the time the order was passed from one warrior to another, the sense of it had been lost before it reached the man for whom it was intended?"

"Yes," said Blackfish, frowning as he tried to see where this was leading.

"Well, these markings represent your words. They do not change as the paper is handed from one man to the next, and once you and the man to whom you wish to give an order or a message both know the secret of the markings, the message will remain unchanged no matter how many hands it passes through."

"Truly?" said Blackfish. "That is a very interesting concept."

"Truly," replied Boone. "And to prove what I say, I will ask Pompey to read General Washington's message to you. If there is any doubt that these are General Washington's own words, I will read it to you after Pompey has finished, and you will see that not a word has changed."

I hope, he added mentally. *There's always the chance that we might translate it using different words.*

Blackfish turned to Pompey. "You will tell me General Washington's message."

Pompey held up the letter and read:

"'To the honorable Blackfish, Chief of the Shawnee nation:

"'Greeting, great Blackfish. The bearer of this message, Daniel Boone, is an old and trusted friend. Twenty-five years ago he and I fought side by side at the Battle of Fort DuQuesne and in subsequent battles as well.

"'Today my country finds itself engaged in the greatest battle against the greatest enemy of all—the British Empire. There is no question that we shall win the war, but we are always hoping to gain new allies to fight for our cause. Daniel has assured me that there are no greater warriors than the Shawnee, and I should be proud and grateful to have you fight by our side against these oppressors.

"'Yours very truly, General George Washington.'"

"Hah!" shouted Girty, slapping his hands together. "He's losing, and he's begging for help!"

"We're not losing," said Boone. "We are gradually driving the British from our land, and when we're through you will be hanging from the highest tree we can find." He turned to Blackfish. "It will be a glorious battle, my father, and you can make a powerful ally. Should the British or the French or the Spanish or any enemy tribes threaten you, the army of the United States of America will fight at your side."

"They're a thousand miles away!" scoffed Girty. "Any war we have with another tribe would be over before Washington even hears of it—and that's if he really means to keep his word and come." He turned to Blackfish. "I urge you to consider this very carefully. If you do not honor this request, neither side is your enemy. But if you fight on the side of General Washington, you have made the British your enemy forever."

Blackfish looked from Girty to Boone, then stood up. "I will consider General Washington's proposal and give you my decision. You are free to leave my lodge until I call for you again."

"How long will that be?" asked Girty. "An hour? A day?"

"As long as it takes," answered Blackfish.

That was the best answer they were going to get, so the three men arose and walked out into the open, followed by the half-dozen warriors. Girty went off by himself, and Boone and Pompey walked some two hundred yards away.

"Do you think he'll do it?" asked Pompey as Banshee flew off to grab a little snack on the wing.

"He'd better," said Boone grimly.

"I don't understand."

"I received *two* letters from Washington," he said, pulling a folded note out of a different pocket. "Here's the other."

Pompey unfolded it and read it.

Dear Daniel:

I have heard of your exploits, and suffered with you through your many trials and tribulations, so much so that I almost hate to write this letter, but I have no choice.

As you know, I have been the commander of the Continental army since it was formed. We have met the British in pitched battles up and down the length of our new country, from Massachusetts and New York in the north to Virginia in the south. What you may not know is that they have been methodically decimating our forces for the past two years. We have the will, but we simply do not have the weaponry to match what the British have. We have begun manufacturing cannons to meet them on land and ships to fight them on the high seas, but it will be years, perhaps decades, before our production equals our needs, and frankly we cannot hold out that long. I have failed three times to recapture Manhattan, and each time my losses have been devastating.

Which brings me to the purpose of this letter. I know that you are the adopted son of Blackfish, chief of all the Shawnee. If you can persuade him to send a few thousand of his warriors to fight for our cause, it will not only be an immediate help but might also convince others of our native tribes to join in the battle against England. I know it is a lot to ask of a man who has given so much already, and I would not be doing so if the situation were not desperate.

Yours very truly,
George Washington

"Would the Shawnee really make that much difference?"

"There are no better warriors," said Boone. "They use the terrain better than any white man I ever saw, and they're as accurate with their arrows as most men are with rifles. Yes, I think a force of a few thousand would have an immediate impact. And if they go, maybe the Mohawks and the Iroquois and some of the other tribes might be encouraged to join them."

"They'd be more likely to try to kill each other," suggested Pompey.

Boone shook his head. "All their battles are territorial. Put them on territory they've never had any claim to and my guess is that they'll fight side by side."

"Maybe I'll suggest to General Washington that every slave he frees will promise to join the army," said Pompey, only half-jokingly.

"I don't think he has the power to free the slaves," replied Boone, "But it couldn't hurt to suggest it."

"What will happen if Britain wins?"

Boone shrugged. "Military occupation. Conscription. Higher taxes. Confiscation of property of everyone who took up arms against them. Public executions of Jefferson, Franklin, the Adams boys, and the rest."

"And Washington?"

"They never kill an enemy commander who surrenders," said Boone. "It's not considered civilized. They'll probably offer him a commission in the British army, and when he refuses, banish him to one of the Caribbean islands."

"I didn't know you'd fought with him," said Pompey.

"It was a long time ago," replied Boone, as Banshee, thoroughly sated, flew back and came to rest in his accustomed spot on Boone's shoulder. "He was just a colonel then. And the Battle of Fort DuQuesne that he mentioned?

We lost it. We were part of General Braddock's outfit, and Braddock turned down the offer of help from Shingas, the chief of the Delawares. It was a lesson Washington never forgot; that's why he sent me here. When you're fighting for your life, you take any help you can get."

"What is he like?"

"Washington? He's a good soldier and a good man. If we win this war with the British, I imagine we'll offer to make him king—and if I know Washington, he'll patiently explain that he just finished winning a war so that we'll never have to have a king again."

"I think I would like him," said Pompey.

"I think you would."

"Maybe, if Blackfish sends his warriors, I'll go along. They'll need someone to translate for them, and I'd very much like to meet General Washington."

Boone glanced back at the chief's lodge, where Blackfish had just emerged. "We'll find out soon enough," he said, starting to walk back to the lodge.

Blackfish waited until Boone, Pompey, and Girty were all standing in front of him, then turned and led them into the lodge, where the seating arrangements were the same as before, and the six warriors took up their positions once again.

"I have considered General Washington's request," he said, "And it is my decision to come to his aid."

"You're making a big mistake!" said Girty harshly.

Suddenly Girty found the naked blade of a knife pressed against his throat, held in the hand of the warrior who stood directly behind him.

"You do not give orders to the great Blackfish when you are a guest in his council house," said the warrior sternly.

No one moved for a long moment. Then the warrior stepped back and Girty noticeably relaxed, his face drenched in sweat.

"To continue," said Blackfish as if nothing had happened, "I will send two hundred warriors under your
command, to be used in whatever way your General
Washington sees fit. In exchange, I will expect General
Washington to send his warriors to my aid whenever I
request it."

"Two hundred?" said Boone, frowning.

"If you feel the offer is too generous, take only one
hundred and fifty," said Blackfish.

"I think you do not fully understand the situation,
my father," said Boone. "General Washington has already lost close to seven thousand men this year alone.
The British forces number almost thirty thousand and
reinforcements are on the way. Two hundred men, even
such brilliant warriors as the Shawnee, simply will not
make a difference. I think General Washington had in
mind something more like four or five thousand warriors."

"And who would be left to defend our land should the
Miami or the Cherokee invade us?" said Blackfish. "Two
hundred is my offer. Two hundred it shall remain."

"You will not change your mind?"

"I will not."

"Then I must refuse your offer, my father," said Boone.
"You would just be sending them off to their deaths."

"What greater goal can a warrior have than to die in
battle?" responded Blackfish.

"Winning that battle."

"Very well," said Blackfish. "The offer is withdrawn. I
will give you safe passage back to the river."

"Wait!"

They all turned to see who had spoken. It was the warrior who had held the knife to Girty's throat.

"Gray Eagle," said Blackfish by way of introduction.
"My oldest son."

Gray Eagle stepped forward. He was a lean, muscular young man who looked neither gray nor like an eagle.

"My father," he said, "Even I have heard of this General Washington. He is a mighty warrior and an honorable man who has never taken up arms against us, and has now asked for help. It will bring shame upon us if we ignore his request."

"You heard me and you heard Sheltowee," said Blackfish. "I offered help and he refused it."

"He refused it because it would not change the outcome of the war," said Gray Eagle. "Neither will any of the other tribes, for none of them will send every warrior they possess."

Blackfish studied his son's face. "Have you an alternative plan?"

"Possibly," replied Gray Eagle. "The tribe that turns the tide of battle will be the most favored, in war and trade, by the Long Knives, is this not so?"

"Yes," said Blackfish irritably. "But I will not risk all of my warriors for that privilege."

"You may have to risk only one," said Gray Eagle. He placed his thumb on his chest. "Me."

"Explain."

"For years we have heard rumors and legends of great dragons who live far to the west, dragons who are bigger than mountains, and able to level whole forests with one breath of flame."

"So?"

"Such creatures could change the course of the war, could they not?"

"If they exist," said Blackfish dubiously.

"Fairy tales!" said Girty contemptuously.

"Perhaps," interjected Boone. "But I've heard those stories too."

"Could such beasts win the war?" asked Gray Eagle.

"If they exist, and if we can find them, and if we can train them, and if we can get them back to the battle-field . . ."

"And if my aunt had balls, she'd be my uncle," snorted Girty contemptuously.

Before anyone could stop him, Boone's right fist shot out and made contact with Girty's jaw. The bearded man was unconscious before he hit the ground while Banshee fluttered in midair, hissing nervously.

"I'll go with you, Gray Eagle," said Boone.

"Do you know the likelihood of actually finding such creatures?" said Pompey in English. "Or of bending them to your will if you do find them?"

"The alternative is to go home empty-handed," replied Boone in the same language. He turned to Blackfish. "May I have safe passage to accompany Gray Eagle beyond your western border?" he asked in Shawnee.

He could almost see the old man's brain working behind the expressionless exterior. If he sent Boone home, Washington would know that he refused to help, whereas if he allowed Boone and Gray Eagle to hunt for these mythical dragons, he could reasonably point out that Boone had refused his offer of warriors and he, Blackfish, was doing everything he could to accommodate Boone and, by extension, General Washington. Another consideration was that Gray Eagle was his favorite son and chosen heir, and if the dragons didn't exist (and he was sure they didn't), then his son would return home safely, without having to fight in the Long Knives' war.

"You may have safe passage, Sheltowee—and there will be no penalty for hitting the man Girty. It is a just punishment for his having the temerity to tell me what to do." He nodded to two warriors, who dragged the unconscious man from the lodge.

"Thank you, my father," said Boone.

"Protect my true son, Sheltowee," said Blackfish, getting to his feet. "And now our business is concluded."

"Not quite," said Pompey.

"Oh?" said Boone, staring at him curiously.

"You two are going to run across a lot of tribes that don't speak English or Shawnee," he said. "I figure you're going to need a translator."

Boone nodded thoughtfully. "I reckon maybe we will at that."

CHAPTER FOUR

They spent the night in Blackfish's camp. Gray Eagle was ready to set out at daybreak, but Boone insisted on creating three chariotlike carts to be pulled by a trio of Landwagons, the one-ton dragons that various tribes, including the Shawnee, had domesticated.

"I thought speed was of the essence," complained Pompey as he labored over the creation of his cart.

"So is survival," replied Boone, hewing a section of a tree trunk into some semblance of a wheel.

"You're not going to expect me to believe at this late date that you have an aversion to walking," said Pompey.

"I like walking."

"Well, then?"

"The Landwagons are grass eaters," said Boone. "Banshee here eats insects. The Nightkillers eat meat. If these giant dragons exist, who knows what they eat? We're taking the Landwagons in the hope that whatever they eat, it isn't other dragons, that they'll just accept them—and us—and let us approach as close as we want. And if we're wrong, then I have to think a two-thousand-pound dragon will look a lot tastier than a man."

Pompey stared at him for a long moment, then smiled. "Perhaps luck wasn't the only reason you've survived out here for so long."

"Speak Shawnee," said Gray Eagle, looking up from his cart. "I cannot understand what you and Sheltowee are saying."

"We'll speak Shawnee when you're around if you'll call me Daniel," said Boone.

"But your name is Sheltowee."

Boone shook his head. "That is your father's name for me. I do not feel like a big turtle, and once we leave this camp I will not answer to the name."

"My father will take offense."

"I won't tell him if you won't," said Boone.

Gray Eagle considered the proposition, and finally nodded his head. "It shall be as you say, Sheltowee."

"Daniel," Boone corrected him.

"Sheltowee now, Daniel once we begin our quest."

"Fair enough," said Boone.

It took them two days to build their crude carts. Since the Landwagons were already broken to the harness, all they had to do was hitch the carts to the big beasts, and load their sleeping mats and personal gear into the carts, and they were ready to leave.

"Which way?" asked Pompey.

"Due west until the sun sets," answered Boone. "And then repeat the procedure until we reach the dragons we want or the Pacific Ocean, whichever comes first."

"Can your friend Washington hold his ground long enough?"

"George is an accomplished pessimist," said Boone. "He's held out for years against the greatest military ever assembled."

"How many men must he face?" asked Gray Eagle.

"I don't know," replied Boone with a shrug. "Maybe thirty thousand, maybe more. But it's more than numbers. The British are the best-trained, best-equipped force in the world. And Washington is holding them off with farmers, merchants, and backwoodsmen."

"He must be a great warrior, this Washington," offered Gray Eagle.

"None better," agreed Boone. "A brilliant man, brave as they come. But a pessimist."

"What does this mean—this 'pessimist'?" asked Gray Eagle.

Boone held up his canteen and shook it, so the Shawnee could hear the water slosh around. "An optimist would say this canteen is half full. A pessimist would say it's half empty."

"Ah," said Gray Eagle, nodding his head.

"And Washington would want to know who pissed in it," added Boone in English, eliciting a laugh from Pompey.

The forest thinned out after a few hours, making traveling much easier, though each man still got a jolt every time his crudely carved wheel turned over the rough terrain. Banshee decided he liked Pompey, and alternated between riding on Boone's shoulder and on Pompey's.

They stopped in early afternoon to give the Landwagons a rest. Boone pulled a piece of jerky out of his pack, cut it in three pieces, and offered a piece to each of his companions.

"It's filthy!" complained Pompey.

"Give it back if you don't want it," said Boone. "I'm sure you can fill up on grubworms."

"I'll eat it," muttered Pompey. "But it's filthy."

"Were slave rations better?" asked Boone.

"When I was a slave, they fed me, they cared for me, they educated me, they—"

"They *owned* you."

"Yes, well, there are flaws in every endeavor."

"Many tribes take slaves in battle," offered Gray Eagle. "Why should warriors do the work of women?"

"Why not just let the women do it?" asked Pompey.

"And turn them into slaves?" asked Boone with a smile.

"Slavery is a terrible thing," said Pompey. "But there's always been slavery and there always will be."

"I don't believe in slavery," said Boone.

"But General Washington owns slaves, and so does Mr. Jefferson, who wrote the fine-sounding Declaration of Independence."

"They're decent men," said Boone. "They'll come around."

"After how many of my people die in chains?" said Pompey.

Boone sighed deeply. "I really don't know. Soon, I hope."

Pompey looked unconvinced.

Banshee, back from another insect hunt, flew up to them and finally perched on Pompey's shoulder.

"See?" noted Gray Eagle. "You have lost his affections, Daniel."

"I'm not that lucky," said Boone. "He'll be back."

"Where did you get him?" asked Pompey.

"One day he just showed up," said Boone. "It was during the siege of Boonesborough, in which I will generously assume Gray Eagle did not participate."

"I was too young," said the Shawnee bitterly. "Blackfish would not permit me to fight."

"I would like to think that's why you're still alive," said Boone with a smile. "Anyway, one day Banshee simply showed up. We'd taken our share of casualties and the corpses were crawling with insects, but even after he'd cleaned them up and had his fill, he stuck around—and he's been with me ever since."

As if on cue, Banshee fluttered over to Boone, who held out a forearm and let the little Darter perch on it. Boone stroked it gently for a moment, then got to his feet.

"We've let the Landwagons rest long enough. We've got a lot of ground to cover."

"No one knows how great their stamina is," remarked Gray Eagle. "We use them in the fields, not on extended trips."

"Then we'll be the first to find out," said Boone, walking to his cart.

Gray Eagle and Pompey followed suit, and the three began heading to the west again. After an hour Gray Eagle called a halt.

"What is it?" asked Boone.

"I cannot do this any longer," said the Shawnee. "Riding in the cart is more painful than anything that can happen to me on foot."

"It *is* uncomfortable, Daniel," said Pompey.

"All right," said Boone. "It's the Landwagons we need, not the carts." He climbed out of his cart and began cutting it loose. "Gray Eagle, has anyone ever ridden these particular Landwagons?" he asked.

"No," answered the Shawnee. "But I have seen men ride Landwagons in war, so I know it can be done."

"They're so big and we're so small by comparison that there shouldn't be much problem. They've been properly broken, and we'll still be giving them the same signals through the reins."

"We can try," agreed Gray Eagle, climbing lightly to the back of his Landwagon, which gave no indication that it even felt his presence.

Boone pulled out his knife and cut the reins much shorter, then tied them together, then waited while his two companions did the same. In a few minutes all three men were mounted.

"It feels awkward at first," said Boone, "but I think if you position your feet atop the wings, you'll have an easier time balancing."

The wings hadn't lifted these beasts in a thousand generations, but they were still there, vestigial, a bright red, clearly a sexual display since they no longer served any other purpose. Boone got his feet set, then clucked gently to his Landwagon. It began plodding forward, followed by its two companions.

"You cost us three days, Daniel," said Gray Eagle. "We should have begun like this, instead of wasting all that time building those carts."

"You'll feel differently tomorrow," said Boone.

"Why?"

"Because the carts could have held the remains of any meat animals we killed."

"The Landwagons can carry them."

"I know that."

"Then I don't understand."

"Each night we'd have buried the meat, and left the carts a few hundred yards away from our camp, just in case Nightkillers got the scent of the meat. But without the carts, if you sling the meat over a shoulder or have your Landwagon carry it across his withers, you'll attract Nightkillers to yourself or your mount. And since we can't spare either of you, that means we're going to have to go on a hunt every time we want meat, and what we don't eat gets left behind."

"You might have mentioned that before we left the carts behind and cut the reins," said Pompey.

"Would either of you have kept your cart?"

"No!" said Pompey and Gray Eagle in unison.

Boone smiled and urged his Landwagon on. The beast trudged forward, grabbing a mouthful of tall grasses every few strides. It was so incredibly placid and docile that it hardly seemed like a dragon at all, surely not when compared with the predatory Nightkillers or even the energetic and inventive little Darters like Banshee.

And yet the land on both sides of the Ohio River was filled with Landwagons, so while he'd never seen them under attack he knew they must have some means of defending themselves. It certainly wasn't speed, and their wings hadn't been functional in millennia. They could probably do a little damage with their powerful legs, but they were so ponderous that any predator could see a kick coming in ample time to avoid it.

Boone shrugged. Sooner or later, probably sooner, one or more of their Landwagons was going to be attacked by Nightkillers, and he'd have ample opportunity to see just what it was that kept them so numerous. A large fly lit on his Landwagon's neck, and drew blood an instant later, just before Banshee turned it into a midafternoon snack, so it clearly wasn't a matter of an impervious skin. Maybe, he reflected, they just tasted bad. He'd heard some men of science offer that same opinion about humans: They survived among bigger, stronger, faster predators simply because they smelled bad and tasted worse. Boone sniffed the air and couldn't detect any odor at all; that was when he noticed for the first time that his Landwagon didn't sweat.

A shadow flickered across his face and he looked up to see a long, lean creature with a ten-foot spread of wings flying past, followed by a dozen more.

"Longgliders," he said, shading his eyes. "Heading southwest."

"Now *there's* a dragon that knows how to make use of its wings," said Pompey.

"They're just scavengers," said Boone. "The *real* king of the sky is the Skyraider."

"But they're barely half as big."

"The Longglider can fly for a day or more without ever touching down," said Boone. "But there's a reason for that. He's got the lightest, hollowest bones you ever saw. See that big one there, the one leading the pack? He probably doesn't weigh fifty pounds. If he swooped down and grabbed Banshee, he probably couldn't take off again. But the Skyraiders—they can fly off with a seven-year-old boy and carry him up to a mountaintop to eat at their leisure."

"I've never seen one," admitted Pompey.

"The Cherokee and the Illini found they were defenseless against arrows, and they killed thousands of them off. They still exist, but there are fewer than there used to be, and they tend to give men a wide berth."

"I wonder if the Longgliders have spotted something to eat—something they might lead us to."

"They haven't."

"How do you know?"

"If they were looking for dead animals, they'd be circling high above us, riding the warm thermals," put in Gray Eagle. "The leader is flying with a purpose, and his family follows. They are probably moving to new hunting grounds."

"Scavenging grounds," Boone corrected him. "Either that, or they're tired of catching arrows in their bellies."

Gray Eagle shook his head. "The Shawnee do not kill the flying dragons, and we are still in Shawnee territory. No other tribe would kill anything on our land."

"What about killing them in your sky?" asked Pompey.

Gray Eagle looked at him but didn't feel that the question deserved an answer.

They rode in silence for another hour, and then Gray Eagle, who had been riding in front, held up a hand.

"What is it?" asked Boone softly.

"Elk," replied the Shawnee, pointing to the barely visible spoor.

"How long ago, do you think?" asked Boone.

Gray Eagle dismounted, examined some crushed grasses, a nibbled shrub. "Ten minutes. Maybe only five." He pointed. "She went this direction."

"She?" asked Pompey.

Gray Eagle nodded. "Only males mark their territory. There are no marks."

Boone looked ahead. "She's probably right in that little patch of bush," he said, indicating some heavy shrubbery some eighty yards ahead.

Gray Eagle nodded. "At least she went in. She may have gone out the other side."

"Ride around and see. I'll give you a minute and then approach from this direction. If she's gone, give a holler; if not, we'll have her trapped."

"We'll make less noise on foot," said Pompey, preparing to dismount.

"Stay on your Landwagon," said Boone. "They may make more noise, but it's the right kind of noise. It won't frighten her off."

Gray Eagle headed off, and disappeared behind the bushes a moment later. Boone spent the time loading his rifle, then urged his Landwagon forward. He'd gone half the distance when he heard a savage war cry from Gray Eagle. An instant later the panicked elk broke out of the bush and raced straight toward him. He took careful aim, squeezed the trigger, and almost fell off his mount from the recoil. When he'd regained his balance he saw the elk lying still, ten yards from him.

They cut off the choicest meat from the loins, lit a fire, and made camp for the night.

"That was excellent," said Pompey when they were through eating. "Nothing could stop me from sleeping tonight."

"You're sure of that?" asked Boone, amused.

"Absolutely." Then: "Why?"

"Because something's sure as hell going to try," said Boone, peering into the darkness. "The smell of our elk has attracted six Nightkillers."

"Seven," Gray Eagle corrected him.

Well, thought Boone, as shadowy figures darted into and out of the moonlight, *at least we'll get to see how the Landwagons protect themselves. And if they don't, then we've got a hell of a long walk ahead of us.*

CHAPTER FIVE

The flames of the fire flickered lower and lower as it began dying.

"Soon," said Gray Eagle, staring into the darkness as he sat cross-legged with his rifle across his lap.

"What if they come for us instead of the Landwagons?" asked Pompey, nervously fingering the trigger of his weapon.

"They won't," said Boone. "There's seven of them, and probably some babies a few miles from here. We wouldn't make enough of a meal."

"You'd better be right," said Pompey.

"He is right," said Gray Eagle.

The three men fell silent for a few moments. Then Boone turned to the Shawnee. "Did you ever see one of your Landwagons come under attack?"

"By Nightkillers?" asked Gray Eagle.

"By anything."

"Almost never," replied the Indian. "They work in the fields, pulling plows and carrying harvests—and we do not cultivate the fields until all the local predators have been eliminated."

"You never use them in war?"

"No."

"Well, it's damned curious," said Boone, staring at the Landwagons, who were illuminated in the moonlight as they grazed contentedly two hundred yards away.

"What is?" asked Pompey.

"You know there are Nightkillers out there. I know it. They have to know it."

"So?"

"So why are they grazing and ignoring them? Why aren't they uneasy, or huddling together for comfort? I didn't hobble mine. Why doesn't he bolt and run?"

"You know, that *is* curious," agreed Pompey. He turned to Gray Eagle. "Have you any explanation?"

"Perhaps they are not frightened," replied the Shawnee enigmatically.

"Not a chance," said Boone. "If you're a grass eater, you know from birth that you're *someone's* dinner."

The three men waited patiently for something to happen—but none of them, not even Gray Eagle, who had lived with Landwagons most of his life—was prepared for what finally transpired.

Suddenly there was a savage scream, half growl and half hiss, and a pair of Nightkillers, each two hundred pounds of sinew and fury, leaped from the shadows for the nearest of the three Landwagons.

The huge beast tensed, opened his mouth, and belched out a blue flame that shot a dozen feet, engulfing both of the predators in fire. One uttered an earsplitting hiss and began jumping in place, throwing itself on the ground, each leap a little less vigorous, until finally, still aflame, it lay on the ground, twitching and then not moving at all. The other one took off for parts unknown, a fireball disappearing in the distance.

Boone glanced back at the Landwagon. It was again grazing on tall grasses, as calmly as if nothing had happened. He couldn't swear that either of its companions had even raised their heads to see the cause of the commotion.

"The others have gone," announced Gray Eagle.

"I can't say that I blame them," replied Boone. "You never saw a Landwagon do that before?"

"Of course I have," said Gray Eagle, repressing a smile.

"Then why the hell didn't any of you Shawnee ever tell me?"

"We thought the great Daniel Boone knew everything."

"Someday I must tell you and your father what I think of the Shawnee sense of humor," said Boone.

Pompey grinned. "I feel a little more confident about hunting for the *big* critters now."

"Well, it certainly explains why Nightkillers don't frighten them," said Boone. "I wonder how in blazes the Shawnee and other tribes ever domesticated them."

"Perhaps it was because we do not mistreat or threaten them," suggested Gray Eagle.

"Some Indian somewhere must have spooked one," said Boone.

"Perhaps," said Gray Eagle. He smiled. "Do you think he'd be in any position to tell us about it?"

"Point taken," said Boone.

Pompey began spreading his bedroll. "I don't imagine we're going to see any more Nightkillers this evening. I don't know about you, but I'm going to sleep."

"Do you mind if Daniel and I talk?" asked the Shawnee. "I have some questions to ask him."

"Be my guest," said Pompey. "If it's interesting enough to keep me awake, maybe I'll join in."

Gray Eagle turned back to Boone. "Blackfish said you have been to the biggest city of the Long Knives."

"That is true," said Boone. "I was in New York four years ago. I guess that's even bigger than Boston or Philadelphia these days."

"Is it as big as Blackfish's lodge?"

Boone smiled. "You have seen the fort at Boonesborough?"

"Yes."

"Imagine one hundred forts and one hundred lodges. New York is still far bigger."

Gray Eagle stared at him for a long minute. "We are both sons of Blackfish," he said sternly. "You should not lie to your brother."

"I am not lying, Gray Eagle," replied Boone. "It is truly that big."

Gray Eagle considered Boone's answer. "Tell me about cities," he said at last.

"What do you wish to know?"

"If a city is that big, it must be because it is filled with men," said Gray Eagle reasonably. "What is it that attracts so many men?"

"There are many reasons," answered Boone. "They live together for mutual defense. The more men, the more guns. They live together because they like to associate with each other. They live together so that each can specialize."

"I do not understand this last."

"It means you can learn to do one thing very well, better than if you had to do many things, and your friends and neighbors will benefit from it, just as you will benefit from them," said Boone. "Let me explain it this way. You, Gray Eagle, are a warrior. But you are also a hunter.

And you supervise work in the fields. And I presume you train Landwagons. And now you are going off on a quest with me. But what if all you did was hunt? And if the man who lived nearest you did nothing but wage war? And the man closest to him only supervised the fields?"

"I would be killed by my enemies, the warrior would starve, and the supervisor—"

"Wait," interrupted Boone. "What if you hunted for all three families, and did nothing else? And the warrior protected all three families and did nothing else? And the man who tended the fields provided the grain and corn for all three families but did nothing else?"

"We would die the first time an enemy attacked," answered Gray Eagle, "for we would have only one man to defend us instead of three."

"What if instead of three of you, there were three thousand, or thirty thousand? What if there were so many that you had enough men to defend you even if only every third or fourth man was a warrior? Do you see the advantages? You could be a much more productive hunter if you did not have to concern yourself with fighting or farming, and so on."

Gray Eagle seemed lost in thought for a moment. "There is something to what you say," he acknowledged. "So the city is divided into warriors, hunters, and farmers?"

Boone smiled again. "No, it is divided into many more things than that."

"I thought so," said Gray Eagle. "Tell me about the other men."

"There are teachers, so that the children grow up to be smarter than the parents. There are doctors, to make the people healthy if they become sick. There are printers and goldsmiths, gunmakers and cabinet makers . . ."

"Does not the father teach the son?"

"There is too much to learn, and the father would have no time to do anything else if he were to properly teach the son," answered Boone. "But if one teacher can teach forty children, he frees forty fathers to do other things."

"I see," said Gray Eagle. "It is a most interesting concept." Suddenly he stared at Boone. "If cities are so wonderful, why do you not live in one?"

"Cities are wonderful for city folk," answered Boone. "I'm not one of them. I like to do my own hunting and my own fighting and even my own farming. And my children will learn what I want them to know, not what some teacher I've never even met wants to teach them."

"I thought so," said Gray Eagle. "Cities take away a man's skills and make him too dependent upon others."

"I've always felt that way," admitted Boone. "But don't forget that there are millions of men, here and in Europe, who disagree."

"And it is this England that makes war upon General Washington in Europe?"

"Yes."

"Then your General Washington will win, with or without our help," concluded Gray Eagle.

"It's possible," said Boone dubiously. "But he's got a lot of city folk in his army, so I think we'd better keep looking for the giant dragons."

"Ah," said Gray Eagle, nodding. "I *knew* there was a reason."

"Any more questions?" asked Boone.

"No," said Gray Eagle. "I will consider all that you have told me. Then I may have more questions."

"Sounds good to me," said Boone, spreading out his bedroll.

It seemed like he had just closed his eyes when Pompey was prodding him with the toe of his moccasin.

"Wake up, Daniel!" said Pompey's voice urgently.

"What is it?" asked Boone.

"We've got company."

Boone rubbed his eyes, surprised that it was morning already. "Did the Nightkillers come back?"

"We're not that lucky," said Pompey.

CHAPTER SIX

Boone sat up and found himself facing six Indians, all
armed with spears and bows and arrows, though none
were threatening him with their weapons.

One of the Indians said something in a tongue Boone
had never heard before. Gray Eagle replied in Shawnee,
and it was obvious that they didn't understand it. Boone
tried English, and the warriors tried another tongue,
both to no effect.

Finally Pompey spoke in French, and they all smiled.

"We come in peace," said the one who seemed to be
their leader, in fluent French.

"What tribe do you belong to?" asked Boone, whose
French was rusty but passable.

"The Dakota."

"Where did you learn French?"

"From the French trappers to the north of us."

"You're a long way from home."

"We got tired of fighting the Cavedancers," said the warrior, "and we are scouting for a new home for our people."

"For *all* the Dakota?" asked Boone.

The warrior shook his head. "Only for my lodge. Perhaps one hundred men and women." He looked over to the Landwagons. "These dragons," he said, indicating them. "Will you trade them to us?"

"No, we need them," answered Boone. "What are Cavedancers—another tribe?"

The six warriors looked at him as if he were crazy. "You have never heard of Cavedancers?"

"Maybe I would know the term in English or Shawnee," said Boone. "But since you don't speak either, perhaps you will tell me what it is that makes an entire lodge of warriors look for new territory?"

"The Cavedancers are huge dragons—flesh eaters who dwell within caves, and come out only to hunt."

"Huge?" said Boone, unable to hide his interest.

The warrior nodded and raised his spear. "As tall as the tip of my spear," he said. "As broad as four men. They can run like a deer, and fight with the strength and savagery of an entire pack of Nightkillers."

"Do they fly?" asked Pompey.

"They have wings, but I have never seen one fly."

Boone turned to Gray Eagle. "What do you think? Are these the dragons we seek?"

"I have no idea," answered Gray Eagle. "I cannot speak the language you are using, so I do not know what they are saying to you." Then: "I am the chief's son. It is not right that I be the only one who cannot understand what is being said."

"I'll translate for you," said Pompey, moving closer to him so he could speak to Gray Eagle without interrupting the others.

"How about you?" Boone asked Pompey. "Do these sound like what we're looking for?"

"They don't sound amenable to training," replied Pompey.

"Nothing does, until you try." Boone turned back to the warriors. "How far have you come?"

"We have marched for nine days."

"Did you see any Cavedancers along the way?"

"Not for the last six days."

Boone waved a hand behind him. "The Shawnee own all the land from here to the big river, the one that the Long Knives call the Ohio," he said. Then he pointed south and west. "I don't think anyone's claimed the land in that direction. At least, no one's gone to war over it."

"And where do three men of different colors go?" asked the warrior.

"Where you came from," answered Boone. "Will the Dakota let us come in peace?"

"We make no war on the white men." He stared at Pompey, then reached out gingerly and touched his hair. "I have heard of black men, but I have never seen one before." He turned back to Boone. "What do you want of the Dakota?"

"Nothing," said Boone.

"Then why do you travel north?"

"To find the Cavedancers."

"Good," said the warrior. "Broken Nose will reward you with a tribute for every one you kill."

"Broken Nose is your chief?"

"Yes—and a very wise chief. Other chiefs make war upon the French or the English or neighboring tribes— but Broken Nose makes war only on the Cavedancers."

Boone resisted the urge to ask who was winning. Winners didn't go on forced marches to seek out new homelands hundreds of miles from where they had been living.

"Tell them," said Gray Eagle to Pompey, "that I am the son of Blackfish, paramount chief of the Shawnee, and that if any Shawnee challenges their right to cross our territory, they are to reply that Gray Eagle has promised them safe passage."

Pompey conveyed the message. The Dakota thanked him, and they seemed about to leave when the leader turned and walked over to Boone.

"I have heard many stories about a white man who became the son of Blackfish, who walks all the way to the great sea without tiring and fights with the courage of a Cavedancer. You are Daniel Boone, are you not?"

"I am Daniel Boone," confirmed the white man.

"I will tell my sons that I stood this close to you and spoke to you."

"I am pleased that you think your sons would care," replied Boone.

"They will care," the warrior assured him. "If I did not feel the need to find a new homeland for our women and children, I would go back and hunt Cavedancers with you."

Boone decided that their true plan would be too complicated to explain, so he simply thanked the warrior. A few more farewells were murmured, and finally they were on their way, leaving Boone, Pompey, and Gray Eagle alone.

The three of them reverted to speaking in Shawnee, and Pompey described the Cavedancers to Gray Eagle.

When he was done, Boone turned to the Indian. "What do you think, Gray Eagle?"

"I do not believe these are the dragons of legend," he replied with conviction. "They are not so huge that they blot out the sun."

"Are you sure the dragons we want are that big?"

Gray Eagle shrugged. "Who knows? Legends have a way of growing bigger with each passing season. If these creatures are as formidable as the Dakota say, then they may indeed be what your General Washington needs."

"Then it's decided," said Boone. "We'll head north toward the Black Hills that I've heard so much about, and we'll see if there is any way we can utilize the Cavedancers against the British."

"It doesn't sound likely," said Pompey. "Twelve feet high, stronger than a pack of Nightkillers, and they spend their time hiding in caves, where they have every advantage over anyone who enters. How do you even approach one?"

"Carefully," said Boone with a smile.

Pompey ignored the facetious reply. "I'm being serious, Daniel. Maybe a handful of these dragons can chase a village of Dakota out of their homes, but tens of thousands of armed, trained British soldiers?" He grimaced. "And how are we going to get the damned critters to the battlefield? We're a long way from Lexington and Concord."

"So is Washington," said Boone. "The British drove him out of there almost two years ago. That's why I'm here."

"He's expecting an awful lot from one lone backwoodsman," offered Pompey.

"Whatever I've got is his for the asking," replied Boone.

"You really think that much of him?"

"I do."

"Why? Just because you fought beside him for a few months? Hell, you've fought beside lots of men, and you wouldn't lay down your life for any of the them."

"He's got a bad deal, and he's never complained," answered Boone. "The Adams boys created this revolution.

Sam was always a rabble rouser, and that Boston Tea Party had his footprints all over it. And John—John's the one who got the Continental Congress to declare independence."

"I thought it was Mr. Jefferson," said Pompey.

Boone shook his head. "Jefferson wrote the Declaration, but it was Adams who proposed it and then rammed it through the Congress."

"You sound like you'd rather not be free of England."

"Makes no difference to me," said Boone. "I can go years without seeing a Redcoat. But I'm an American, so when they say to fight for my country, I'll take up arms and fight. But I'm just one man. Look at Washington's situation: Half the people don't want to break away from England. Half of what's left want independence but don't want to go to war over it. But Congress declares independence, and suddenly Washington's out there on the battlefield with a bunch of untrained and ill-equipped troops, outnumbered and outgunned, while Adams and Jefferson and Franklin and the rest sit around in Philadelphia passing resolutions. I was on Long Island in New York when Washington was trying to put together his army a few years back, and I'll tell you the truth—Blackfish could have led five hundred Shawnee against all three thousand of Washington's men and won by nightfall. And Washington wasn't preparing to fight five hundred half-naked Shawnee; he was getting ready to face fifteen thousand battle-hardened Redcoats with at least that many more on the way." He paused, trying to ease some of the tension from his body and voice. "And you know the interesting part? He's never once complained. Never once. He's asked for reinforcements, sure, who wouldn't—but he's never suggested that they gave him an impossible task, not because he's the best general we've got, which he is, but because they knew no one else would accept it."

"He's held his own for a few years now," noted Pompey.

"He is a great warrior," said Gray Eagle. "His deeds are known even to the Shawnee."

"He knows he can't take the British head-on," continued Boone, "so he's letting his men shoot from behind bushes and rocks. Clever plan, but he's losing. You know it, I know it, he knows it, and the British sure as hell know it. That's why we've got to find some way to put the dragons to use. This is our land. They inhabit it. They can help fight for it."

"Perhaps the dragons will fight," Pompey conceded. "But how do you ensure that they attack only the British and not Washington's men?"

"I'm a frontier legend," said Boone with a sardonic smile. "I'll find a way."

"I hope so," said Pompey, "because I figure our life expectancy can be measured in minutes once we finally run into these Cavedancers."

"What do *you* think, Gray Eagle?" said Boone.

"Nightkillers, Redcoats, Cherokee, Cavedancers, it's all the same to me," said the Shawnee. "I'm a warrior. If I survive this adventure, someday I will become the war chief of the entire Shawnee nation. It would be good to form an alliance with your General Washington against the British and the French."

"And the Spanish," added Boone. "I hear they're making inroads."

"The Indians do not hunger for the Long Knives' land," said Gray Eagle. "Why do they have such a great hunger for ours?"

"Most of them could not own land in England," answered Boone. "They came here because the British promised them land."

"*Our* land."

Boone nodded. "Your land."

"That is why we must help General Washington kill the British."

And when that's done, thought Boone, *you'll kill every American who's sitting on Indian land, which means anywhere on the whole damned continent. But we'll worry about that when the time comes. Our first job is to defeat the British.*

Aloud he said: "Let's pack up and get moving. The sooner we find these Cavedancers, the better."

Washington can't wait forever, he reflected. *And from the sound of his letters, forever could come next month.*

CHAPTER SEVEN

They trekked north and west for six days. Game was plentiful for the first four days, but then it became so scarce that they were reduced to eating such fruits as they could find. Boone and Gray Eagle had no problem adding grasshoppers and the edible bark of some trees to their diet, but Pompey would not partake of them.

On the morning of the seventh day, all signs of animal life had vanished, yet there was no evidence of drought or fire.

"Have you noticed?" mentioned Gray Eagle. "Not only is there nothing moving on the land, but there are no birds, no Longgliders, no Skyraiders."

"I've noticed," replied Boone.

"What does it mean?" mused Pompey.

"If it means what I think it means, we've wasted a week," said Boone. "And I don't know how many weeks Washington can spare."

"I don't understand," said Pompey.

"It looks like Cavedancers are everything those Dakota said they were," said Boone.

"How can you can say that?" persisted Pompey. "You've never even seen one."

"I don't have to," replied Boone. "All I have to do is look around me and read the signs. All the game that could flee the area *did* flee it. Nothing's left."

"Maybe they're just hiding."

Boone shook his head. "They're hiding, all right, but not around here. There are no Nightkillers, no other predators of any kind. No scavengers, either. Look up in the sky. There should be Skyraiders circling up there, looking for food. There should be Longgliders trying to spot carrion on the ground. But there's nothing. That means that the Cavedancers have cleaned out all the game, and if that's the case, there aren't enough of them to turn the tide of war."

"How do you reach that conclusion staring at an empty plain and sky?" Pompey demanded. "There could be Nightkillers all over. Maybe they have the wisdom to hide, so as not to get burned by our Landwagons."

Gray Eagle stared at him. "You can read and write, but you cannot *see*."

"I didn't see the same damned things *Daniel* didn't see. I just want to know how he can make these assumptions."

Boone stopped to light a hickory pipe. "Let's take a break," he said, sitting down. "I don't like to walk and argue at the same time."

"I'm not arguing," said Pompey, sitting down a few feet away as Gray Eagle followed suit. "I'm *asking*."

"The Cavedancers are the most efficient killers in the territory, maybe in the world," explained Boone. "But that can be a bad thing."

"How?"

"They're obviously not very fast," said Boone. "They haven't run any game down."

"How do you know?" demanded Pompey.

"No sign," said Gray Eagle. "Even if a Cavedancer ate the entire animal, including the bones, we would know from the spoor what had happened. But there is no sign of a hunt, no sign of any kills."

"And from that, we know the Cavedancer is a stalker, not a chaser. He's not built to catch animals on the open plain. He uses strength to kill, not speed. And that in turn means he's stuck here. He's not going to cross the river, and he's not going out on the open plains where the deer and the buffalo can see him coming and race away from him."

"I still don't see how that leads you to say that we've wasted a week. If they don't travel, at least we know where to find them."

"You still don't understand," said Boone. "Look around you: The game is gone. I'll bet it's been gone for years. And there are no scavengers."

"What do scavengers have to do with anything?" asked Pompey in exasperation.

"The Cavedancer is the king of the predators, at least in this territory," said Boone. "And when you're the king, you eat the choicest parts of your kill and leave the rest for your subjects, which is to say, for the scavengers. But game is so scarce that the Cavedancers are eating *every* part of their kills—hooves, horns, bones, everything. There's no sign of any scavengers, no dragons anywhere in the sky. That means it's been a long time since game was plentiful enough for the Cavedancers to just eat the good parts and leave the rest for the scavengers. And *that* means that there's not enough food to go around. We knew that already, from the Dakota we met; animals don't hunt armed men unless their normal food isn't available." Boone paused. "Can you come up with the answer now?"

"I may not know the wilderness like you two do, but I'm not stupid," said Pompey. "I can come up with two answers, and they both mean the same thing. First, if the Cavedancers have started putting men on their menu, we're going to have a tough time convincing them that only Redcoats are good to eat. And second, if they won't leave the area to follow their food supply, they sure as hell aren't likely to march a thousand miles to the battle-field just because we tell them to."

"Right on both counts," agreed Boone. "But you still haven't seen the most obvious fact."

"Enlighten me," said Pompey.

"There probably aren't enough of them left to make a difference," said Boone. "There are usually about a hundred grass eaters for every flesh eater. Now almost all the local grass eaters have left. The Dakota are starting to leave. How the hell many Cavedancers can be left? They're such successful killers that they've run out of things to kill, and that means they've run out of things to eat." He turned to Gray Eagle. "Tell him what happens to a race of animals—any kind of animals—when they run out of food."

"They starve, and they stop reproducing," said Gray Eagle.

"Right," agreed Boone. "So the ones that haven't starved to death aren't making little Cavedancers. Even if we could train them, and even if we could march them to the coast without their feeding off Americans, how much difference do you suppose they'd make to a well-armed force of thirty or forty thousand Redcoats? How many Cavedancers can there be left in these parts? Fifty? A hundred? Two hundred?"

"It's no wonder the Dakota are looking for a new place to live," said Pompey. "I could get awfully sick of berries, and I don't even eat grubworms and the other disgusting things that seem to delight your palate. The Cavedancers haven't left them anything else—unless Cavedancers are good to eat and there's a way to kill them."

"If you look hard enough, there's a way to kill anything," said Boone.

"Why look?" said Pompey. "If you're right about the Cavedancers, we're wasting our time here. Why don't we just leave?"

"Because most of the Dakota haven't left."

"This is their homeland," said Pompey, "Not ours. Let them worry about how to survive next to the Cavedancers."

"They *are* surviving, or they'd have joined the small party we met," answered Boone. "Everything I've told you is logical—but dragons don't always follow the rules of logic. Maybe the Dakota know something we don't know yet. If it's how to kill them, then we'll change course and head west, and hope these weren't the dragons that the Shawnee have heard rumors about . . . but if it's how to *control* them, well, maybe we can put them to use after all."

"I thought there weren't enough of them."

"There aren't—*here*. But this isn't the only territory with caves and forests. Maybe there are only a hundred Cavedancers left in the world, and maybe there are tens of thousands just in America. If it's the latter, we owe it to Washington to at least find out if they've learned to control them."

"All right," acquiesced Pompey. "It makes sense." Suddenly he smiled. "I wonder if George Washington ever thought he might be commanding a brigade of Cavedancers."

"I doubt that he's even heard of them," said Boone. "The colonies are getting civilized. There were three different types of grass-eating dragons that used to dwell there—two in the Carolinas and one in Delaware—and we managed to kill every last one of them." He shrugged. "They wouldn't know what to do if they saw a Cavedancer."

"Will you?"

"Run, I suppose," said Boone with a smile. "Or climb the nearest tree."

"I have never seen Sheltowee run," commented Gray Eagle.

"If you don't remember to call me by my Christian name, you'll see me run all right," said Boone, still smiling. "Right after you, with a tomahawk in my hand."

"I am sorry, my brother," said Gray Eagle. "Sometimes I forget."

Suddenly Pompey looked up into the sky. "Daniel—I thought there weren't any flying dragons in the area. But I'm looking at maybe sixty Longgliders."

Boone glanced at the flying wedge. "They're not scavenging, Pompey," he said. "They're migrating."

"How can you tell?"

"Did you ever see sixty Longgliders looking for food in the same place? They're heading west. Even with the wind against them, they'll go another three hundred miles before nightfall." He paused, then added wistfully: "I'd sure like to see what's out there."

"You may get your wish," said Gray Eagle. "I do not think the Cavedancers are the dragons of legend. Once we have made sure, we will continue our quest."

"I'd like to meet Broken Nose and see if he has heard of any other race of dragons," said Boone. "And if we run into any French trappers, they should be all too happy to help us once they know we're fighting the British."

"I've heard Blackfish speak of Broken Nose," said Pompey. "He thinks Broken Nose is a good chief." He paused. "Part of it may be that the Dakota have never made war on the Shawnee."

Suddenly Boone let out a curse.

"What is it?" asked Pompey.

"Banshee," muttered Boone. "He's digging his claws into my shoulder." He pried the little dragon loose and placed him on the ground, where he huddled against Boone's thigh.

"He's trembling," noted Gray Eagle.

"I've never seen him like this," said Boone. "Something's scaring him."

"I don't like the sound of this," said Pompey nervously. "How many things in the vicinity could scare him?"

Boone reached for his rifle and opened his powder pouch as Gray Eagle did the same thing.

"Can you see him yet?" asked Boone softly.

"No," replied the Shawnee.

The Landwagons began getting as nervous as Banshee.

"He's scaring the hell out of them," noted Pompey, "and they stood off a whole pack of Nightkillers without flinching."

"Tether them," ordered Boone. "We can't have them bolting at the wrong time, or in the wrong direction."

The three men dismounted and tied the Landwagons to some small trees.

"Hobbles would be better," said Pompey. "They can burn down the trees whenever they want."

"Let's hope they're too dumb to think of it," answered Boone, scanning the area. "Well, wherever the hell he is, he's going to have to cross fifty yards of flat ground. That ought to be enough."

"It wasn't enough for those Dakota we met last week," said Pompey nervously.

"We have guns," said Boone. "They had spears."

"I hope your guns are loaded," said Pompey, as some instinct urged him to look off to his left. "Because we aren't alone anymore."

CHAPTER EIGHT

By God, he's impressive!" murmured Boone as he got his first look at a Cavedancer and the Landwagons began squealing in terror.

The dragon wasn't shaped like any other he'd ever encountered. It was about ten feet in length, and stood about as tall as a Landwagon—but just as he was convinced that the Dakota had exaggerated its height, the dragon rose up on its back legs, and seemed every bit as comfortable walking on two legs as on four.

Its skin was brown and covered by scales that glistened in the sunlight like a snake's. Its tail seemed short for its body, and was used as a balance as it slowly approached them.

The head was formidable. The mouth held close to one hundred long, razor-sharp teeth. The nostrils were proportionately larger than those of the Landwagons, which implied that it had an excellent sense of smell. The ears, too, were large. *But of course they'd be*, thought Boone; *if it lives in caves, it needs some well-developed senses besides vision.*

The eyes were huge, totally out of proportion to the rest of the head, but just from the way it constantly tested the air and the way it kept turning its head, listening, Boone decided that it couldn't see very well in the daylight. Those eyes were made for the minimal light of caves and dark spaces. If he'd had any warning, any description other than that it was ferocious and awesome, he could have simply moved downwind of it. He had a feeling that the Cavedancer couldn't tell him from a tree stump in bright daylight, and flesh eaters didn't charge tree stumps.

All this Boone recognized and cataloged for future use in the first two seconds. The trick now was to survive so he could put these observations into practice at a later date.

"If he gets close," he said softly, trying to keep his voice calm so as not to alarm or irritate the Cavedancer, "keep clear of those front legs. He'll be trying to grab you with them."

"To hell with his feet," muttered Pompey. "Look at those teeth!"

"Pay attention," said Boone. "He won't come after you with his teeth. He'll use those claws on his front feet. Those teeth can rip off any piece of meat they find. That means he doesn't need his claws to do it—and there's only one other reason for a flesh eater to have claws. If he wasn't going to use them, he'd still be on all fours."

"The heart," said Gray Eagle, looking down the barrel of his rifle. "Right or left, high or low?"

"You take the right, I'll take the left," said Boone. "Pompey, go for one of the back legs, as close to a joint as you can get. If we can't kill him, let's at least see if we can slow him down."

The Cavedancer turned to the squealing Landwagons, seemed to briefly consider approaching them, but then turned his attention back to the men.

"Right now?" asked Pompey, lining up his shot.

"No," said Boone. "Let him get closer."

"Damn it, Daniel—he's only fifty feet away!"

"We don't know anything about him except the obvious," said Boone. "We've got to make our shots count."

"I'm not going to miss anything that big at fifty feet!"

"I never said otherwise," replied Boone. "But we don't know how thick his skin is. We've got a lot better chance of hitting something vital at ten feet than fifty."

"Ten?" gulped Pompey as the Cavedancer continued his slow, almost leisurely, approach.

"Ten," said Boone. "If nothing else, the force of the bullets ought to knock him down and give us a few seconds to think of something else."

"Daniel!" whispered Gray Eagle. "Left jaw, just below the eye."

Boone looked and saw a newly healed wound. It could have been from a prey animal. More likely, given its length, it was caused by a battle with another Cavedancer. "Well, at least we know their skin can be cut open. I wish you'd brought your bow and arrows."

"It wouldn't do any more harm than a bullet," said Gray Eagle, never taking his eye off the Cavedancer.

"No, but if it was sticking out of him, he'd be as apt to spend all his energy on *it* as on us. If he can't see the enemy buried in his flesh, he'll go after the next best thing, which is us."

The Cavedancer came to a halt thirty feet from them, moving its head slowly from side to side. This was beyond its experience. Every living thing ran from it. These three creatures stood their ground. The Cavedancer wasn't stupid, but it had developed to hunt in a certain way prey that reacted in a certain way. Sometimes it caught its prey and sometimes it didn't, but no prey animal had ever even considered standing its ground, and it could not come up with a response.

So it stood and stared, hissing softly, waiting for one of the men to break into a run so it would know what to do.

"What's going on?" whispered Pompey.

"He's confused," said Boone. "Don't make any sudden movements and we might just get out of this without firing a shot."

It almost worked. The three men and the Cavedancer stood and stared at each other for a full minute. Boone could feel some of the tension seeping away from him—and then it happened. A butterfly fluttered by, about four feet to Boone's right—and suddenly Banshee hissed and flew after it.

Movement! That was what the Cavedancer had anticipated, what it had been waiting for. Now it finally knew what to do. It opened its mouth and emitted an earsplitting sound that was half hiss and half roar, a sound that usually terrified its prey into temporary immobility.

Pompey squeezed the trigger of his rifle. Boone could hear the *thunk!* as the bullet hit the back leg just below the hock joint, could see the dust rise at the point of impact. The Cavedancer screamed and turned toward the source of the sound.

Pompey began furiously reloading his weapon. Boone realized that with the profile the Cavedancer was presenting him, he could easily take out the beast's eye—but he also knew that it wasn't using its eye, so instead he concentrated on the likeliest location for the heart, and fired.

The Cavedancer staggered for a moment, then turned and leaped toward Boone. Boone was momentarily startled at the speed with which the wounded dragon was able to move, the ground it could cover leaping on a shattered hind leg. He threw himself to his left, and the beast's talons missed him by inches.

"His skin's too tough!" shouted Boone. "Try something else!"

"You! Dragon!" cried Gray Eagle, hurling a dagger into the Cavedancer's snout. "The son of Blackfish has no fear of you!"

Boone kept rolling, making sure he was clear of the dragon before he stopped to see what was happening. Gray Eagle was keeping up a stream of invectives, and every time the Cavedancer looked toward Boone or Pompey the Shawnee hurled a rock at it.

Finally the dragon turned its full attention to Gray Eagle. It approach him fearlessly, and when it was five feet away it opened its terrible jaws and reached out for the Indian with its talons. That was the moment Gray Eagle was waiting for. He shoved the barrel of his rifle into the Cavedancer's mouth and pulled the trigger.

The back of the Cavedancer's head flew off, blood and brains shot into the air, and the creature fell to the ground, its forelegs twitching spasmodically for another fifteen seconds before it lay still.

Boone got to his feet and walked over to stare at the body. "Well, that's one way to get past the skin," he said.

"So then how did he get the scar below his eye?" asked Pompey.

Boone pulled out his hatchet, knelt down next to the Cavedancer's head, wedged the handle in its mouth until he could separate the massive jaws, and then brought the hatchet down on the teeth with all his strength. The resultant *clang!* could be heard half a mile away. All Boone got for his effort was a very sore arm. The teeth were completely unmarked.

"There's your answer," he said to Pompey. "A Cavedancer's teeth may be the only thing that can leave that kind of scar on a Cavedancer's skin." He got to his feet as Banshee finally returned to his shoulder, then tucked the hatchet back in his belt while wishing his arm would go numb so it would stop hurting.

"These creatures are *formidable*," said Pompey. "I wonder if there's any way to capture and transport them, and then turn them loose behind the British lines."

"Don't be foolish," said Boone. "Even if they were as formidable as you seem to think, we'd need thousands of them. This war will be long forgotten before anyone can capture that many—if indeed there are that many still alive."

"You think they're *not* formidable?" demanded Pompey.

"We're three men and we killed one of them. Do I have to keep telling you how many troops the British have?"

"But you and Gray Eagle are very special men with very special knowledge of how to fight these things," said Pompey.

"Two bullets slowed it down. Enough will kill it, even if you don't stand your ground and fire into its mouth. But the British won't settle for bullets. They've got cannons. This is a tough animal, but it can't stand up to a cannon." He paused. "Still, it's one hell of a dragon."

"No wings on this one," noted Gray Eagle.

"Not all dragons have wings," answered Boone. "And even with wings, the only ones that can fly are the Darters, the Skyraiders, and the Longgliders."

"That we know about," put in Pompey.

"That we know about," Boone agreed.

"So what now?"

"I don't think the Dakota can point us to anything more formidable," answered Boone. "Tomorrow we'll head south and west and hope this isn't the only kind of dragon that we didn't know about."

"Why tomorrow? There's nothing keeping us here."

Boone and Gray Eagle exchanged looks.

"All right," said Pompey. "What am I missing."

"We're in Cavedancer territory," said Boone. "Who knows how far west it extends?"

"So?"

"So as long as we've got a willing subject, we're going to take it apart and see where its vulnerable parts are, how best to get to them in case this isn't the only Cavedancer we encounter."

"So I'm a scholar, not a hunter," said Pompey with a shrug.

"You're also a pretty good shot," said Boone, walking around the corpse. He pointed to the blood-soaked back leg. "You didn't hit the joint, but you shattered the bone just below it."

"Then how could it keep on its feet?"

Boone shrugged. "We won't know until we cut it open. My first guess is that it can tolerate a lot of pain."

"What's your second guess?" asked Pompey.

"That it's never *felt* any pain and didn't know how to react to it."

"What do you mean, how to react to it?" demanded Pompey. "You react by collapsing."

"Have you never had some pain that didn't make you collapse?" asked Boone.

"Yes, but I know what precautions to take."

"Well, it didn't," said Boone. "Pain—this kind of pain, not what it would consider the equivalent of a little scratch under its eye—was a new sensation. It didn't know not to walk on a shattered leg, that it would just make things worse. Eventually the leg wouldn't have held its weight, but it probably wasn't thirty seconds from when you shot it to when Gray Eagle killed it."

"You know," said Pompey thoughtfully, "I've read Shakespeare, and I've read Chaucer, and I can speak three languages and about a dozen dialects, but I suddenly realize that my education has been sadly lacking."

"Well, let us investigate this beast," said Boone, pulling out his knife and hatchet, "or you may get another lesson sooner than you'd like. We've still got about four hours of daylight."

"What's the hurry?" asked Pompey. "There aren't any Nightkillers in the area. We know that."

"There's not much of *anything* in the area," said Boone. "And it's been my observation that when they run out of grass eaters, most flesh eaters will turn cannibal before they starve. I have no objection to turning this Cavedancer over to his hungry kin, but I'd like to be long gone before it happens. Most flesh eaters are scavengers when they have to be, but they do tend to like their meat fresh if given the opportunity."

Pompey instantly knelt down next to the carcass, knife in hand.

"Where do I start?" he asked.

The stoic Gray Eagle actually laughed.

CHAPTER NINE

They headed south for two days, then turned west. There was no particular reason to think Gray Eagle's legendary dragons lived to the west, but if they existed at all, they certainly hadn't been found in the other three directions.

"How far do you reckon it is to the Pacific Ocean?" Boone asked Pompey five days into the westward trek as their Landwagons stopped to graze.

Pompey shrugged. "I'm not sure. None of the maps I've seen are that accurate. My best guess is that we're still closer to the Atlantic."

"Then we've got a lot of ground to cover," said Boone. "I hope Washington can hold out." He grimaced. "Hell, he could have surrendered a month ago and the news wouldn't have reached us yet."

"If these damned Landwagons were a little more responsive maybe we could cover that ground a little faster," complained Pompey. "It's hard to control them with just a halter. I don't know why we can't saddle and bridle them like horses."

"Their mouths aren't built like a horse's," replied Boone. "There's no place for a bit to fit."

"Ben Franklin isn't the only inventor in the country. Someone could create a bit."

Boone smiled. "How long do you think it would take a Landwagon to melt it?"

"I forgot," admitted Pompey. "But that still doesn't explain why we can't have saddles."

"Those shriveled little wings work just as well," Boone pointed out. "Why go to the trouble of making saddles and stirrups?"

"But its skin keeps moving and twitching. I'm getting sore in a place where no man wants to get sore."

"Ride sidesaddle."

"Thank you, Daniel," said Pompey sourly. "I appreciate your sympathy."

Boone pointed to a herd of buffalo grazing about half a mile away. "You could always ride one of them if you're tired of Landwagons."

"You're just full of helpful suggestions today," replied Pompey.

Gray Eagle pointed to a spot far in the distance. Boone peered at it for a moment, then turned to the Shawnee.

"Fire?" he said. "If it is, and the herd stampedes toward us . . ."

Gray Eagle shook his head. "I don't think it's a fire."

"Smoke signals?"

The Shawnee nodded. "The land is flat. The smoke can be seen as far away as a two-day march. It's the easiest way to talk to one another."

"It can't be about us," said Pompey. "They can't even know we're here yet. We're still too far away."

"No, it's not about us," agreed Boone.

"What do you suppose it means?"

"I don't know," answered Boone. "It could be anything from a declaration of war to the equivalent of a lunch chime. But at least it means there's someone we can ask about the dragons we're looking for."

"Maybe we should make sure they're friendly first," said Pompey.

"Fine. Send them a smoke signal saying that we come in peace."

"I don't know how."

"You start by lighting a fire."

"Spare me your sarcasm," said Pompey. "I may be a linguist, but no one ever taught me how to converse in smoke."

"Then we have two choices," said Boone. "We can alter our course and circle around them, but that could add a few days to our journey and there's no guarantee that we won't ride right into more members of the same tribe—or of a rival tribe, for that matter. Or we can ride straight ahead and have a powwow with them." He looked around. "I don't suppose there's a settlement of white men within four hundred miles, so there's every likelihood that they'll never have seen a black man *or* a white man. If they don't know who or what we are, they have no reason to fight with us."

"I don't know about that; some people are just hostile," said Pompey, pulling out his gunpowder and starting to load his rifle. "Just in case," he explained when he saw Boone and Gray Eagle staring at it.

Boone offered no comment, but urged his Landwagon forward. The dragon finished chewing the mouthful it was working on and then began plodding in the direction of the smoke. Once Boone's beast was in motion, the other two followed suit.

"We'll use sign language to start with," said Boone, "But I want you to pick up whatever tongue they speak as fast as you can. I want to know if they've heard anything about the dragons we're looking for."

"Maybe we'll get lucky," said Pompey hopefully. "Maybe they'll be between here and whoever's sending the smoke signals."

"If they are, then they're not flesh eaters," said Boone.

"What makes you so sure?"

"Take a look at the buffalo," said Boone. "They wouldn't be grazing that calmly if there was anything around that was likely to eat them. They'd post a number of lookouts around the outskirts of the herd, and they'd be lifting their heads, testing the wind, every few seconds."

They rode for three more hours, passing still more buffalo, and finally they were able to see a cluster of wigwams in the distance.

"Have you ever seen any domiciles like that, Daniel?" asked Pompey.

"Once or twice," said Boone. "Makes it easier for them to pack up and move the whole village."

"Why would they?"

"If they were farmers, they'd stay put. But the land's not cultivated, at least not as far as I can see," replied Boone. "That means they're hunters, and they'll move their village to follow the game. When the buffalo graze the area out and move on, so do they."

"It makes perfect sense when you say it," admitted Pompey. "But I could look at the same thing and never come to that conclusion."

Boone smiled. "I could try to read a book of Greek or German and never understand a word of it. We do what we're trained to do."

A party of a half-dozen Indians began riding out of the village to meet them, and Boone noticed that whatever they were riding was a little smaller and a lot more nimble than the Landwagons. He turned to Gray Eagle.

"Have you ever seen anything like that?"

Gray Eagle shook his head. "No."

Pompey, whose eyesight was not as keen, peered at the oncoming Indians. "Horses?" he asked.

"Dragons," said Gray Eagle. "See how the sun glints off their scaled skin."

"And the buffalo are paying no attention, so they're used to them and know that they're grass eaters," said Pompey, looking quite proud of himself.

Boone smiled. "The buffalo are going to break and run to the south any second now."

And almost as the words left his month, the entire herd suddenly took off to the south, bellowing and grunting.

"Then they *are* meat eaters?" asked Pompey.

"No," said Boone. "But they're being ridden by meat eaters. This herd has been hunted before. They didn't pay any attention when the dragons came into sight, but the second they caught wind of the Indians they panicked."

Pompey sighed deeply. "There's a lot you don't learn growing up on a plantation," he said.

Soon the Indians were close enough for Boone's party to see their mounts.

"Blue," said Boone, frowning. "Gray Eagle, have you ever seen a blue dragon before?"

"Never," answered the Shawnee.

Suddenly a prairie dog raced across the path of the lead dragon. Startled, the dragon jumped high and to its right, landed without losing a beat, and continued approaching Boone.

"Nimble as all get-out," said Boone. "I wonder what we should call them?"

"How about Blue Nimbles?" suggested Pompey.

"Why not?" agreed Boone. "It's as good a name as any, and probably better than some."

Gray Eagle continued staring at the dragons. "No wings," he said at last.

"Not all dragons have 'em," said Boone.

"No saddles either," continued Gray Eagle, obviously for Pompey's benefit.

"No guns, which is a lot more important," said Boone, shading his eyes and peering across the plain. "You know," he continued, "it's possible that they've never seen a rifle before. If things get tense, fire a shot into the air. The noise might be all we need to scare them off."

"If they don't have any guns, how do they kill the buffalo?" asked Pompey.

"With arrows and spears," said Boone. "Or maybe with the Blue Nimbles."

"I thought you said these particular dragons weren't flesh eaters."

"They're not," answered Boone. "But that doesn't mean that once a buffalo scents their riders they can't run him down until his heart bursts. Anything as light on its feet as these Blue Nimbles usually isn't lacking in stamina. One of the things that tires an animal out is the pounding his legs take when he's running."

The lead Indian raised his hand in the universal gesture of peace, and Boone responded in kind.

When the two groups were fifty yards apart the Indians slowed their mounts down to a fast walk.

"They look friendly enough," observed Pompey.

"I hope so," said Boone. "I'd love to trade our Landwagons for what they're riding."

The two groups stopped when they were perhaps twenty feet apart.

"Tell them we come in peace," said Boone.

Pompey repeated the message in English, French, Shawnee, Miami, and Illini. There was no indication that the Indians understood him.

Then the lead Indian spoke. Pompey shook his head. The Indian spoke again, and Pompey again indicated that he couldn't understand him. The Indian tried once more, and this time Pompey smiled and responded.

"What language is that?" asked Boone. "It sounds vaguely familiar, like I've heard it somewhere before."

"Believe it or not, it's Cajun."

"Cajun?" repeated Boone. "What the hell is he doing speaking Cajun?"

"Hold on and I'll ask," said Pompey. A moment later he got his answer, and turned to Boone. "He's got a Cajun squaw," he said. "Evidently her family disapproved of the man she wanted to marry, so she ran off with him and wound up out here in the territories. They settled down a few days' march from here and started a farm. Made their peace with these Indians and their tribe, and things seemed to be going well—but four winters ago he came down with fever and died. By then, everyone she knew was an Indian, and her family had already disowned her so there was no sense going back to New Orleans, so finally she married this fine fellow here, and after a while he learned some Cajun. I guess she gave up on French and English. Anyway, he says his name's Fast Rider, and his tribe calls itself the Kiowa."

"Tell him we would like to trade for some Blue Nimbles."

Pompey exchanged a few sentences with Fast Rider.

"He says we have nothing to trade except the Landwagons. He's never seen one before, but his squaw has described them, and he has no use for a beast of burden. Like you said, they're nomads, not farmers."

"All right, then," said Boone. "Ask him if he'd like to *sell* us some Blue Nimbles."

Fast Rider laughed and uttered a brief reply.

"He wants to know what you plan to buy them with."

"Three hundred pounds of buffalo meat."

Another exchange.

"He says he can slay his own buffalo."

"Just as well," said Boone. "No sense showing him what a rifle can do until we have to." Suddenly he grimaced. "Oh, hell, he already knows. His wife will have told him. Well, so much for Blue Nimbles. You might as well ask about the dragons we're looking for."

"I don't know what we're looking for," said Pompey. "Or at least I don't know how to describe them."

"Big," said Boone. "Just get that across—that they're *huge.*"

Pompey cleared his throat and posed the question to Fast Rider, who made a prompt reply.

"We're in luck!" said Pompey excitedly. "He knows something!"

"What?"

"He was a little vague," said Pompey. "Let me ask him again."

Yet another exchange in Cajun.

"He seems perfectly friendly," announced Pompey. "He's even offering us the hospitality of his village."

"But?" said Boone.

"But he figures this information is worth even more to us than the Blue Nimbles were."

"He doesn't want the Landwagons, so what *does* he want?" asked Boone.

"He says he'll think about it while we all ride back to his village for dinner."

"Tell him if he's worried about our passing the information on to others, Daniel Boone knows how to keep a secret."

Suddenly Fast Rider's face became animated. "Daniel Boone?" he said. "Daniel Boone?"

Boone tapped his chest with a thumb. "Daniel Boone."

Fast Rider spoke very rapidly to Pompey, who nodded and turned to Boone. "Your reputation precedes you," he announced. "Fast Rider has heard stories about the famous Daniel Boone from his squaw. He says when we reach the village you can pick out any three Blue Nimbles and they're yours."

"Thank him graciously for me," said Boone.

"He says he is honored to play host to you and your servants," said Pompey with an ironic smile.

"Perhaps tonight I will teach him how to address the son of a chief, " said Gray Eagle grimly.

"He means no harm," said Boone. "Maybe we can get our information tonight and be off at sunrise."

Fast Rider spoke up again.

"Um . . . it's not going to be quite that easy, Daniel," said Pompey.

"He's decided not to tell us about the dragons?"

"He's decided what he's going to charge for it."

"Oh?" said Boone suspiciously.

"After we eat tonight, he wants the great Daniel Boone to take on the best fighter in the village."

"Is it him?"

Pompey asked.

"No, it's not Fast Rider."

"One of the others perhaps?" suggested Boone, appraising each of the warriors in turn.

Another question, another answer. This time Pompey looked positively grim.

"He's not in this group."

"Too bad," said Boone. "We could have gotten it over with right now."

"There's a reason he's not here, Daniel."

"Oh? What is it?"

"He's so big that they don't have a Blue Nimble that can carry him."

CHAPTER TEN

The village, such as it was, consisted of thirty-two wigwams. The Nimble Blues, some five dozen of them, grazed in a pasture a few hundred yards away under the watchful eyes of a trio of teenaged boys. The women were tending a community fire, each in charge of some aspect of it or some item of the communal dinner.

Everything came to a dead halt when Boone and Pompey entered the village. Gray Eagle elicited very little interest. He was just another Indian in a land populated by Indians. But many in the village had never seen a white man, and Boone could tell by their reaction that none of them had ever seen a black man. They crowded around Boone and Pompey, speaking in whispers, occasionally reaching out to touch a hand or a leg.

Finally a deeply tanned dark-haired white woman came out of a teepee. She was dressed in buckskins and she wore a headband, but she walked right up to Boone and spoke to him in English.

"Welcome to my home," she said. "Have you traveled far?"

"A fair distance, ma'am," said Boone.

"They say that you're Daniel Boone," she continued. "Can that be true?"

"That it is, ma'am—and these are my friends, Pompey and Gray Eagle."

"Is this one your slave?" she asked, indicating Pompey.

"I don't believe that men should own each other," answered Boone. "Like I said, he's my friend."

"No offense meant," she said to Pompey. "But I come from New Orleans . . ."

"We know," said Boone. "Your husband told us. But he didn't tell us your name."

"Martha Delacroix," she said, and then smiled. "Or Mrs. Fast Rider, if you prefer."

"You know why we're here, ma'am?"

She nodded. "The giants."

"Have you seen one?"

"No, but I've heard about them."

"Do your people have a name for them?" asked Boone.

"Yes." She uttered a word that made no sense to Boone and his companions.

"Can you translate that?"

"I suppose the closest you can come is Thunderflame."

"So they can spit fire?" asked Pompey.

"I don't know," replied Martha. "As I said, I've never seen one." She paused. "I just hope Mr. Boone lives long enough to see one."

"Is there some reason why he might not?" asked Pompey.

"I heard the women talking about the conditions my husband has placed upon leading him to the Thunderflames."

"I'm pretty good at taking care of myself, ma'am," interjected Boone.

"Under normal circumstances I'm sure that's true," said Martha. "But there's nothing normal about Tall Mountain."

"That's the man I'm to fight?"

"To call him a man is like calling a cyclone a mild summer breeze," she said.

"Even so," said Boone, "it's just to entertain the tribe. It's not a fight to the death, so even if I lose, we'll leave at sunrise."

"I hope so," replied Martha.

"You think Fast Rider might go back on his word?"

"No, my husband would never break his word."

"Then I don't understand," said Boone.

"It might be difficult to ride with two broken arms and two broken legs," said Martha.

Boone looked around the village. "I don't want to seem immodest, ma'am, but I don't see anyone who's capable of doing me that kind of harm."

"He's in his wigwam," said Martha. "That body of his requires an awful lot of food and sleep."

"Well, there's no sense worrying about him until I come face-to-face with him," said Boone. "Let me make sure of one thing: We're here as honored guests of the Kiowa, right?"

"That's right."

"So Pompey and Gray Eagle can walk around freely?"

"Yes."

Boone turned to his companions. "I want you two to wander through the village," he said in Shawnee, so Martha couldn't understand him. "See if you can find out anything about this giant I have to fight, and especially see what you can learn about the Blue Nimbles. If this Tall Mountain is half what the woman says, we may want to leave in a hurry *before* I have to fight him."

"Makes sense to me," said Pompey, heading off.

"I have never seen you run from a fight before," commented Gray Eagle.

"There's a difference between running from a fight and running from a slaughter," said Boone.

Gray Eagle considered his remark, finally nodded his agreement, and went off to wander through the village.

"They won't let you," said Martha when they were alone.

"I beg your pardon, ma'am?"

"They won't let you run off without fighting."

Boone looked surprised. "You speak Shawnee?"

"No, but I'm not a fool, Mr. Boone. I know you were giving them orders, and I know you didn't want me to hear what you were saying. Now, given the conditions, what other orders could you possibly give?"

"Well, it can't hurt to be prepared."

"It won't do you any good, but no, it can't hurt," agreed Martha. "And now may I ask you a question?"

"Go right ahead, ma'am."

"What in the world is the great Daniel Boone doing out here looking for Thunderflames?"

"You know we're at war with the British, don't you, ma'am?" said Boone.

"I know some of you were," she said. "Is it still going on?"

"It's still going on, and it's going badly."

"I'm sorry to hear that. I may not live with my own people anymore, but I'm still an American. But what has a war hundreds of miles away got to do with you being here?"

Boone explained why he and his party needed to bring General Washington as many Thunderflames as they could.

"I've never seen one, but I've heard Fast Rider and a few of the others talk about them," said Martha. "And if half of what they say is true, I don't know how you can get a Thunderflame to go anywhere it doesn't want to go."

"The alternative is to keep losing to the British until there's no one left to fight on our side, ma'am," said Boone. "I've at least got to see for myself that these dragons can't be trained."

"If you survive tonight, I'm sure that's exactly what you'll see," said Martha. "You know," she added carefully, "there is an alternative."

"Oh? And what might that be?"

"Go west and don't even think about the war," she said. "I'm sure you could talk Fast Rider and the others into joining you. We're nomads anyway, so it's nothing to uproot our little community and move it to a new location."

"I can't do that, ma'am," said Boone. "First, I'm an American, and that means I've got to do everything in my power to make the British recognize our new country. Second, George Washington is a personal friend, and I won't let him down. And finally, even if the first two reasons didn't apply, moving west just postpones the day that the British come west to claim the rest of the land. You don't really think they'll be content to stop at the Ohio or the Mississippi, do you?"

"I didn't even know they were still here," she said. "My knowledge of the British military is just about nil, and my knowledge of your General Washington isn't much better."

"Anyway, I thank you for the suggestion, ma'am, but I came out here to find these dragons, and I'm not about to quit now that I've come this close."

"You're a man of fine moral character, Daniel Boone, and I'm sorry I even suggested that you'd do anything besides help your General Washington. If there's anything I can do to help you, let me know."

"There *is* one thing, ma'am," said Boone.

"What is it?"

"My friend Pompey can speak Cajun, but none of us can speak Kiowa. If you hear of anyone planning to break their bargain with us, I'd appreciate being told."

"They're an honorable people," she said. "They'll keep their word."

"But just in case . . ."

"Yes, I will warn you if the situation should call for it, but I promise you it won't. The only warning you need is: Don't fight Tall Mountain."

"If I could find the Thunderflames without the Kiowa's help, I'd have no problem sneaking off right now," said Boone. "But since I don't know where they are, I have a feeling I'm going to have to see this through."

"God protect you, Mr. Boone."

"You can be sure that I'll ask for His help, ma'am," replied Boone.

Gray Eagle approached Boone just then.

"Well?" said Boone, reverting to Shawnee. "Did you learn anything?"

"Two things," replied the Shawnee. "One, all the Nimble Blues are trained and respond to neck-reining. They also respond to verbal commands, but since we don't know the Kiowa tongue, that won't be of any help to us."

"Okay," said Boone. "What's the other thing?"

"A wise man would leave before he had to fight Tall Mountain."

"So I've been told."

"But you will stay," said Gray Eagle. It was not a question.

"I will stay," said Boone.

Pompey joined them a few minutes later.

"How did you fare?" asked Boone.

"Would you believe that no one in the whole damned village speaks Cajun except for Fast Rider and his squaw?" he said in annoyed tones. "I picked up a few words of Kiowa. It's not difficult. I'll be able to make myself understood in about a week."

"Let's hope it doesn't take us that long," said Boone.

Gray Eagle nudged Boone's shoulder and looked across the village. Boone followed his gaze and saw Fast Rider approaching them.

"Are you prepared for dinner?" asked the Kiowa as Martha translated for him.

"I suppose we are," said Boone. He looked around. "I don't see anyone answering to Tall Mountain's description."

"He doesn't eat before he fights," answered Fast Rider. "He feels that the food makes him sluggish."

"That's not a bad idea," acknowledged Boone. "I reckon I'll skip dinner too."

"You are sure?" said Fast Rider. "We have cooked a buffalo calf for you and your friends."

"I'll eat my share *after* the fight," replied Boone.

"Then there is no reason to delay the fight until after dinner," said Fast Rider. He summoned two braves, and the three of them conversed in low tones for a moment. Then he turned back to Boone. "We will have the fight now."

"Are you sure we have to go through with this?" asked Boone. "I have no argument with Tall Mountain, nor he with me. We could just sit by the fire and smoke our pipes."

"For years we have heard stories about the prowess of Daniel Boone," said Fast Rider. "We want to see if the stories are true."

"I was a lot younger when most of those tall tales were born," said Boone. "And that was before I broke my ankle a couple of times. And—"

"Enough modesty," interrupted Fast Rider. "You are the greatest fighter among the white men. Tall Mountain is the greatest fighter in all the Kiowa nation. This will determine who is the greater of the two."

"Have you ever considered that the greatest man is the one who finds reasons not to fight?" asked Boone.

"Never," said Fast Rider so promptly and decisively that Boone didn't need Martha to translate.

"All right," said Boone unhappily. "Let's get this over with."

"Give me your weapons to hold," said Fast Rider.

"Has Tall Mountain given you his?" asked Boone.

Fast Rider actually chuckled. "Tall Mountain needs no weapons."

"I was afraid of that," muttered Boone.

Boone suddenly realized that he was no longer standing in the sunlight. He hadn't noticed any clouds during the day, and he turned to see what had obscured the sun.

He almost wished that he hadn't.

Standing a stride away was the largest man he had ever seen, probably the largest anyone had ever seen. He towered almost two feet above Boone, and more than seven and a half feet above the ground. His shoulders were massive, his chest awesome, his thighs like tree trunks, and yet, despite his mass, he gave the impression of carrying no excess weight. He might have tipped the scales at four hundred pounds, but it was four hundred pounds of bone, muscle, and sinew.

Boone didn't have to be told that this was Tall Mountain. He looked around to see if there was a referee, or if anyone was going to explain the rules of the fight. Before he could turn back, Tall Mountain had reached out and grabbed him by the shoulder as if he were a rag doll.

Boone felt his shoulder go numb. He kicked out with his left leg, caught Tall Mountain full in the belly—and all that happened was that he himself yelped in pain and felt his foot starting to go numb as well.

He reached out with his free hand, extended two fingers, and jabbed Tall Mountain in the eyes. The Indian released his grip and placed his hands to his face as Boone fell to the ground.

Boone gathered himself and hurled his body at Tall Mountain's right knee. It didn't crunch and go soft the way a normal man's would have, but he felt it buckle a bit. The Indian, blinking furiously, reached down for Boone, but Boone scrambled and rolled to the side, then launched himself at the back of Tall Mountain's knees.

The Indian grunted in surprise and slowly toppled over backward. Boone avoided the huge body, then chopped Tall Mountain's exposed Adam's apple with the edge of his hand. The giant began choking and gasping for air while thrashing about blindly with his hands. Boone jumped back out of reach and turned to Martha.

"Ask Fast Rider when this thing is over," he said.

"When one of you can't stand up, or when one surrenders," replied Fast Rider through his wife.

"Ask Tall Mountain if he's had enough," said Boone without much hope.

Tall Mountain was too busy coughing to answer, but his answer was clear enough as he began struggling to regain his feet. Boone hurled himself at the Indian, feet-first, and knocked him over again.

"You can't keep doing that all night, Daniel!" said Pompey. "You're not hurting him, you're just knocking him off balance."

"Of this I am aware," muttered Boone as the giant began getting up again.

"Go for his throat!" shouted Pompey.

There was a difference between hacking at Tall Mountain's throat when he was down and blinded, and going after it when he was upright and ready for an attack. Boone took a look at those massive hands, already reaching out for him, and decided not to chance it.

For the next four minutes he ducked, sidestepped, maneuvered, did everything he could not to fall into that powerful grasp. The only result was that he was four minutes wearier, his twice-broken ankle was smarting, and Tall Mountain wasn't even breathing hard.

He scanned the ground, looking for a barren spot, someplace where he could pick up a handful of dry dirt and fling it into the Indian's eyes, but there was grass everywhere he looked.

He studied the heavily muscled Kiowa, searching for weak spots—and as he was concentrating, he responded a fraction of a second too slowly, and was firmly in the giant's grasp. A roar went up from the assembled Indians as the giant began shaking Boone until the latter felt that he would fly apart any second. He reached for an eye, Tall Mountain turned his head—but in doing so, he exposed the area just behind where his jaw joined his skull. Boone made a fist, extended his thumb, and jabbed at the area with all the strength remaining to him.

The giant dropped like a stone, releasing his grip on Boone, who fell to the side and rolled out of reach.

Tall Mountain got slowly onto his knees, and while has hands were on the ground Boone leaped in and rammed his thumb into the very same spot. This time the Indian didn't move when he hit the ground.

"May I claim victory now?" Boone asked Martha.

He waited for the translation, Fast Rider nodded his assent, and a cheer went up from the assembled Kiowa.

"Now we shall eat," announced Fast Rider.

"You go ahead," said Boone. "I'll be along in a bit." He turned to Martha. "Bring me some cool water and a rag to use on him."

"He lost," said Fast Rider. "Let him lie there."

"He fought for the honor of the Kiowa," responded Boone. "He deserves respect, not contempt."

Martha returned a moment later with the water, and Boone began cleaning Tall Mountain's face, and forcing some water between the huge warrior's lips. After a moment the Indian opened his eyes.

"Did I win?" he asked dazedly.

"You lost," said Boone after the translation.

"I have never lost before," said Tall Mountain. "Daniel Boone is everything they said he was." He placed a massive hand on Boone's shoulder. "You have defeated me in fair combat. I will follow you anywhere."

"Could you tell him," Boone said to Martha, "that I don't need someone to follow me, but I could sure use someone to *lead* me to the Thunderflames."

"It will be my honor," said Tall Mountain, "and I will share it with no other."

He stared coldly at the Kiowa braves. No one volunteered to come along.

"Tell him that my Landwagon will easily carry his weight," Boone told Martha. "He can have it, and my two friends and I will ride a trio of Nimble Blues."

"He agrees," reported Martha. "He says he will be ready to lead you at the first light of day." She paused. "If you have any further questions to ask of him, ask them now, because once you set out tomorrow you won't be able to communicate with him except by sign language."

"Signs will be fine," said Boone. "And if he's willing to talk, point to things and say the Kiowa word, and Pompey will be able to converse with him in a few days."

"Then I'll say goodnight and wish you Godspeed, Daniel Boone," said Martha.

They were off at the first light of the new day, four men with nothing in common except a desire to find the home territory of the Thunderflames.

CHAPTER ELEVEN

Three days into their journey they topped a small ridge and came to a halt.

Tall Mountain pointed ahead.

"My God!" said Boone, staring in awe. "He's everything we hoped he'd be!"

"And more!" said Pompey devoutly.

"He is magnificent," said Gray Eagle.

"I knew we were looking for something big and impressive," continued Boone, "But I never dreamed anything like this could exist!"

"There's just one question," said Pompey. "How in the world are we ever going to make it do our bidding?"

PART TWO

GEORGE WASHINGTON'S BOOK

Chapter Twelve

George Washington looked out across the rolling Pennsylvania hills. His men were camped in a broad semicircle, their tents torn and patched and torn again. He hoped he didn't have to face the British again for at least a week. It wasn't generally known, not even to his own men, but his army had barely enough ammunition for a two-hour pitched battle.

The bright side, he thought with a sardonic smile, was that they might starve to death before they had to fight that battle. Or freeze. Or succumb to disease. He led five thousand men; more than half had marched through the snow with no shoes.

He was a good general, one of the very best. He knew it, and it wasn't immodest to acknowledge that fact to himself. But how much longer could even a good general keep fighting against an overwhelming British force, a force that was equipped with the very best weaponry, that never lacked for food or clothing or ammunition, that had engaged in wars like this all over Europe while he was leading a ragtag band of accountants and clerks and farmers and backwoodsmen?

He'd figured out three years ago that he couldn't meet force with force, firepower with firepower, so he borrowed from the Indians, he hit and he ran, he attacked from ambush, he refused to meet the British in anything resembling a traditional military formation.

He looked at the cup of tea, no longer hot or even warm, that had been sitting, ignored, on his makeshift desk for the better part of an hour. They were so short of supplies it seemed a shame not to drink it. He wrestled with his conscience for a moment and finally downed it with a single swallow. His wooden teeth were hurting again, and he'd tried to stay on a liquid diet, but he had a feeling he was going to need some real food in the morning. Tea and soup might be all right back home at Mount Vernon, but in the middle of a war he needed something more substantial, whether it hurt his gums and jaws or not.

He picked up a quill pen and stared at the blank piece of paper that lay on the desk. It was time to write another report to the Continental Congress. He dreaded writing them, because it had been a long time since he'd had anything hopeful to report. He wrote the missives himself, rather than dictating them, because he didn't want his troops to learn just how dire the situation was. An army can exist when it is short on food, short on shoes, short on firepower—but once it's short of hope, the war is over.

And, he reminded himself, there was still reason to hope. There was a possibility that the French would take a more active hand; not that they cared one whit for the American cause, but rather because they loved hindering the British. Then there was the hope he could join up with the militia led by Elijah Clarke and Andrew Pickens, whose Georgia and Carolina troops had just won a major battle. Of course, it was a battle against a bunch of loyalists, rather than the British army itself, but the early reports were that they'd defeated quite a large number of them, turncoats who had been marching to Atlanta to join up with the British.

And, perhaps least likely of all, there was Daniel Boone. Could his old friend rally the Shawnee and some of the other tribes to fight on his side? And even if he could, would they be enough to change what now seemed to be the inevitable outcome of the war?

Washington hadn't seen Boone in close to a decade. He'd been too busy commanding his forces when they were both in New York a few years ago, but he'd heard about Boone's accomplishments. If any American deserved to be a legend, it wasn't Sam Adams or Tom Paine, who fomented revolution and then let everyone else fight it, but Daniel Boone, who carved out new territory for the infant nation, who started settlements up and down the Ohio and the Mississippi, who had befriended numerous Indian tribes. And whatever his disagreements with the Shawnee, he had nonetheless been adopted by the mighty Blackfish.

The more Washington thought about it, the more he decided that Boone might well be his best bet, rather than his least likely. But where was he? Why had there been no word from him for months now? Just how long did it take to recruit a few hundred Indians?

And suddenly Washington felt deflated again. A few hundred Indians, even a few thousand . . . they might extend the war for a year, possibly even two, but he knew in his heart that they weren't going to make the difference between victory and defeat. It was up to him, and him alone. He'd had some triumphs, far more than anyone had any right to expect, but lately the overwhelming numbers and firepower of the British had simply been wearing his army down. He'd lost a lot of men this year, through death and (he ruefully admitted) through desertion. Attrition could do more damage to an army than cannon fire.

He shook his head, as if to rid himself of negative thoughts. There was no sense dwelling on things he couldn't change. He had a war to fight.

"Sir?"

Washington turned to see a young man standing respectfully at the flap to his tent. "Yes, Mr. Eakins?"

"A message from General Arnold, sir," said Ephram Eakins, saluting and stepping forward. He handed the dispatch to Washington.

"Does it require an answer?"

"I don't know, sir," said Eakins. "I can't read."

"As long as you can aim a rifle, we'll settle for that," said Washington.

"That I can, sir. There were four of us brothers, and we all joined up. My brother Ben was with Light Horse Harry Lee at Paulus Hook up in New Jersey. Ben says we took more than four hundred British prisoners and only lost one man."

"Your brother Ben is correct," said Washington. "There is no better commander than Harry Lee. Did you fight at Paulus Hook too?"

"No, sir," said Eakins. "I joined up at Brandywine, and I've been with you ever since."

"Brandywine," said Washington with a grimace. "That was a poor introduction to war."

Eakins nodded his agreement. "I lost my other two brothers there."

"I am sorry, Mr. Eakins."

"It's war, sir. They died for what they believed in. No one's to blame."

My God! thought Washington. *He's lost two brothers, and he's comforting* me! Aloud he said, "Do your parents know about your brothers?"

"I don't rightly know how they could, sir," said Eakins. "Corporal Mason promised to teach me enough book-learning that I could write and tell them, but lately we've been on the run so much that I ain't had a chance to sit down with him and start my lessons."

"When you do learn, please tell your parents how sorry I am about your brothers, and add that they died bravely."

"That they did, sir," said the young man. "And I'll be sure to tell 'em what you said. They'll be thrilled to hear it from a famous man like yourself, sir."

"Well, let me see what Benedict has to say," said Washington, uncomfortable, as always, when being praised. He tore open the dispatch, took it over to the lamp by his desk, and read it.

"Good news I hope, sir?" said Eakins.

"Not bad news, at any rate," said Washington, finishing the message and setting it down. *Not news at all. Just more of the same. He complains that he isn't appreciated, he tries to poison my mind against his superiors, he hints that the British would know how to treat a man of his gifts, and then he asks me to expand his command to include West Point.*

"Is there any answer, sir?" asked Eakins. "I can come back later for your message if you want to write to him. In the meantime, Lieutenant Barnes is hunting up a fresh horse to carry your dispatch back to General Arnold."

Washington shook his head. "No answer."

"Then, with your permission, I'd best be hunting up Corporal Mason and sneak in a little book learning before the British find us again."

"That sounds like a fair division of labor, Mr. Eakins," said Washington. "You take care of the reading and writing, and I'll take care of the British."

The young man saluted and left the tent, Washington began writing his report to the Continental Congress, and a few minutes later George Rogers Clark entered.

"Am I intruding, sir?" he asked.

Washington looked up from the report. "My generals can never intrude on me," he replied. "Come on in, George. I only have this one chair, but grab a stool and make yourself comfortable—or minimally less uncomfortable, anyway."

"Thank you, sir," said Clark, sitting down.

"What can I do for you, George? Or," he added hopefully, "is there something you can do for me?"

"Maybe a local woman can do something for all of us."

"Not another brothel, George," said Washington wearily. "Half our men have already contracted the disease."

"No, sir, not another brothel," said Clark.

"What is it, then?"

"Sir, there's a woman I think you should meet. She lives on a farm about forty miles southwest of here. Her name's Amanda Blakely. She's a widow. Lost her husband very early on, at Bunker Hill. She has a talent that I think could actually affect the outcome of the war."

Washington looked dubious. "That's a very bold statement, George."

"It certainly is—but I'll stand by it."

"All right," said Washington. "Suppose you tell me about it."

"I'd rather show you, sir," answered Clark. "I have a feeling if I describe it to you, it may sound ludicrous— not her talent, but the use to which I think it can be put. This is something you should see with your own eyes, sir."

"I'm trying to prepare our defenses and our escape routes if—make that *when*—the British attack. And you're asking me to spend a whole day, maybe two, riding forty miles from here to see a talented woman."

"It sounds rather silly when you phrase it like that, sir," said Clark.

"It certainly does."

"Nonetheless, that's precisely what I'm asking you to do," continued Clark. "You've always trusted me before. Trust me one more time."

Washington sighed deeply. "How can I say no when you put it that way?" He paused thoughtfully. "And in truth, we can't afford to overlook any possibility, even one so unlikely that you would feel silly describing it to me. I just hope you don't feel as silly after I see whatever it is for myself."

"I won't."

"All right," said Washington. "We'll ride there at sunrise."

"I think you just might be pleasantly surprised, sir," said Clark.

"It would be nice, just for a change," replied Washington.

CHAPTER THIRTEEN

He'd been expecting a typical farm, with crops in nice neat rows, cattle in a pasture, perhaps some poultry or Darters in a coop as a source of eggs. What he found was something quite different.

Washington had risen with the sun and left immediately after breakfast, accompanied by Clark, young Eakins, and a couple of junior officers. They were riding some of the very few horses that existed on the continent, purchased from the Spanish, and even so the journey had taken them almost two days.

Every now and then Washington would see a shadow fall across the trail. He'd look up and there would be a Skyraider, floating on the thermals or flapping its leathery wings. They all seemed to be heading in the same direction, and he wondered if he was seeing an early migration—but he soon decided that couldn't be the case, since they were all flying alone, or at most in pairs. His second thought was that there must be excellent hunting up ahead to attract so many Skyraiders. He hoped so, since his men could certainly use the meat.

Washington was anxious to pierce through all the mystery and see what Clark had found. Clark seemed nervous too. Only Ephram Eakins seemed happy, as he undoubtedly was. A ride on a horse, a special request for his presence, an ever-increasing distance between himself and the nearest British army . . . what was there not to feel good about? He hummed quietly to himself, and then, without his realizing it, the humming became louder and he began adding the lyrics.

Well, thought Washington, *at least one of us isn't worried.* And yet, this was exactly why he'd brought the young man along. Ephram Eakins was the stuff of the new nation, industrious, honest, brave, all the things the United States would need once it won this war. His lacks were not going to be detriments in his lifetime; one didn't need the gift of literacy to fight or to farm. Or to sing a cheerful song as the little group rode toward the Blakely farm.

The land began getting hilly, and the forest started encroaching in earnest.

Washington turned to Clark. "Are you sure we're going in the right direction?"

"Yes, sir."

"I thought you told me that this Blakely woman lived on a farm."

"She does, sir," replied Clark.

"There are too many hills, too much undergrowth," noted Washington. "It must be damnably difficult to farm here."

Clark smiled. "I suppose it all depends on what you're growing, sir."

Washington was about to reply when a Skyraider swooped down not twenty feet ahead of him and flew off with a small rodent in its claws. Washington's horse reared up, surprised, but was soon under control.

"I think I've seen more Skyraiders today than I've seen since this war began," said Washington. "Probably even longer than that. We don't have many around Mount Vernon." He held a hand up to shade his eyes from the sun. "No Longgliders, though."

"I saw one yesterday, sir," offered Eakins. "Biggest I ever saw. You'd think *they'd* be the ones to be making off with squirrels and the like."

"They're so big that it takes every bit of strength they've got just to lift themselves off the ground," replied Clark. "They can't carry anything even as small as a squirrel or a rabbit. That's why they're the scavengers and the Skyraiders are the killers."

"Skyraiders do a little scavenging, too," Washington pointed out. "I doubt that there's a meat eater anywhere in the world who'll pass up an easy snack that someone else has thoughtfully killed for him."

"I wonder if there's a dragon somewhere that's kind of a cross between the two," mused Eakins. "As big as a Longglider, but as strong as a Skyraider." The young man smiled. "Wouldn't that be something?"

"Anything's possible," answered Clark. "We've only explored a very small part of the continent." He turned to Washington. "I hear that some Spanish clergy have sailed all the way around South America and plan to come north and start a settlement on our Pacific coast. Maybe they'll be the ones to find Mr. Eakins's new breed of dragon."

"I wonder what kind of reception they'll get?" said Washington. "Who knows the manner of man they'll encounter out there?"

"I think we should thank the Spaniards, sir," suggested Eakins.

"Oh, do you, Mr. Eakins?" said Washington, amused at the young enlisted man's brashness, especially compared with the very nervous lieutenants' lack of it. "And why should that be?"

"Sooner or later we're going to settle and own all the land from the Atlantic to the Pacific," said Eakins with absolute certainty. "The more of it they civilize, the less work we'll have to do."

Clark laughed aloud. "He's right, you know," he said.

"*Some*one will settle the continent," said Washington. "There's no question of that. My job is to see that it's us and not the British."

"If we don't beat 'em this time, we'll beat 'em next time, sir," said Eakins.

"No, Ephram," said Washington. "If we lose, if we surrender, the people will be too disheartened to take up arms again."

"Don't you bet on it, sir," said Eakins, who seemed totally unafraid to contradict his commander. "If the British win, that'll be just one more reason to drive them out later."

"If they win, they're going to hang every officer and every member of the Continental Congress, then confiscate every rifle in our new United States, and make it impossible for us ever to go to war with them again," said Washington. "That's why we keep fighting, and that's why we cannot lose."

"We have faith in you, sir," said Eakins. "You'll pull another trick out of your hat, like when you crossed the Delaware and caught them with their trousers down."

"I appreciate your confidence, Mr. Eakins," said Washington. "I hope it isn't misplaced."

More shadows crossed the trail.

"There must be something very large and very dead up ahead," noted Washington. "Every Skyraider within miles seems to be heading directly for it." Then: "How much farther have we to go?"

"Less than two miles, sir," answered Clark.

Washington peered ahead. "Are you sure? The land doesn't seem to level out anywhere within my range of vision."

Clark quickly surveyed his surroundings. "Yes, sir, I'm sure. I've been spotting the proper landmarks along the way."

Washington looked dubious, but said nothing. They rode in silence for another ten minutes, and finally they saw a small, dilapidated wooden house at the top of a tall hill. Nearby was a barn and a trio of outbuildings.

"That's it," announced Clark.

Washington turned to his two lieutenants. "Set out in a pair of semicircles, meet at the house, and see if there's any sign that the British are here or nearby."

The two young men saluted and set off on their routes, joining up just in front of the house, then cantering back.

"It looks safe, sir," said one of them, and the other concurred.

"All right," said Washington. "Let us proceed." He looked ahead. "I don't see any farm animals, George, and the fields haven't been cultivated in at least two years."

"I know."

"And you still insist that visiting this place could mark a turning point in the war?"

Clark was about to answer when the door to the farmhouse opened and a tall, wiry, middle-aged woman, the sun glinting off her spectacles, musket at the ready, emerged.

"State your name and business," she said harshly. "And be quick about it!"

"It's me, Amanda—George Clark."

She squinted through her small spectacles, then lowered her gun. "Welcome back, General Clark."

"May I present our commander-in-chief, General George Washington. General Washington, this is Amanda Blakely."

She performed an awkward curtsy. "General Washington!" she exclaimed. "I thought General Clark was lying or bragging when he said he planned to bring you here. I wish my husband was here to see this!"

"How did you lose him, Mrs. Blakely?" asked Washington.

"He died at the Battle of Saratoga."

"I'm very sorry," said Washington, who found himself saying those words all too often these days.

"Can I offer you and your men something to eat?" asked Amanda.

Washington pulled his mount to a stop about twenty yards from her, then dismounted.

"We thank you for your hospitality, Mrs. Blakely," said Washington. "Perhaps later. We're here to see . . ." He paused. "The truth is that I don't know *what* we're here to see, but I'm sure you can tell me."

"I can do more than tell you, General Washington," she replied. "I can *show* you."

With that she took a small wooden whistle out of a pocket, raised it to her lips, and blew into it.

A moment later they heard a high-pitched hiss from overhead, and suddenly a Skyraider swooped down toward them. It landed atop one of the chimneys, then flapped its leathery wings once and dropped lightly to the ground. It remained there, motionless, ignoring the six humans who stood some ten yards away from it.

"Now watch," said Clark.

Amanda walked over to the winged dragon, which didn't shy away from her or indeed pay any attention to her whatsoever. She lifted a tiny foreleg, a quarter the size of the hind legs, in her hands, and suddenly Washington saw that there was a tiny pouch attached to the leg. Amanda opened the pouch and withdrew a small piece of paper. She unfolded it, read it, and handed it over to Washington.

"As you can see," she said, "one of my cows just produced twins. That's a message from the man who manages my farm."

"I thought *this* was your farm," said Washington.

"This is one of them. The one with my cattle is eighty miles south of here. *This* is where I keep my dragons." She pointed to the barn and the sheds. "I have forty-seven of them."

"Do you see the possibilities?" said Clark eagerly. "We can use Skyraiders to carry messages. They can do in an hour what it might take a man two days to do—and they can fly right over the British positions without rousing any suspicions!"

"I'd love to use them as carrier pigeons. The British would never realize what we were doing—but nothing's ever that easy," said Washington. "Mrs. Blakely, how do the Skyraiders know to fly from one of your farms to the other?"

"They were born here, and this is where they come when they're released," she answered. "Once every month my manager rides his wagon up here and goes back with ten or fifteen Skyraiders. They're used to being handled, and whenever he has a message for me, he attaches it to a Skyraider's leg and turns it loose."

"Do you see the problem, George?" said Washington. "Unless I am to fight the remainder of the war from this very spot, I won't be able to receive any messages."

"Surely they can be trained!" protested Clark. "After all, no one's ever domesticated a Skyraider before, and she's got forty-seven of them!"

"That's all true—but by the time you did train them, the war would be over."

"Let's not be too hasty here," said Clark. "We need every advantage we can get, and these would provide us with an enormous advantage."

"Mrs. Blakely," said Washington, "how long does it take a Skyraider to accept being handled by you or your manager?"

"The ones that we hatch out ourselves are handled every day of their lives and never have a problem with it," she replied. "As for the wild ones . . . some take a few weeks, some a few months, some never."

"How does one acquire wild ones?" asked Washington.

"They see the tame ones flying to one of the outbuildings, they see or scent the food we're giving them, and they show up to beg for their share."

"Interesting, but not very useful," said Washington. "If we can't teach them to seek us out and land at our field headquarters, I just don't see how they can be of any help at all."

"I can teach them a few things," said Amanda. "To let me attach the pouch, to let a human approach, to leave my farm animals alone—but I can't teach them to land at a different spot every day."

"I can," said Ephram Eakins.

CHAPTER FOURTEEN

Eakins's bold claim hung in the air for a moment before Washington turned around to face the young man and ask precisely how he intended to proceed. "Go ahead, Ephram."

"When we were back on the farm in Ephrata—that's in Pennsylvania, sir; it's the town I was named for—we raised all the usual animals: cattle, goats, Darters, chickens, even a few sheep."

"Get to the point, boy!" said Clark.

"Let him tell it his own way, George," said Washington calmly. "His family has paid a high enough price for us to at least grant him that."

"Thank you, sir," said Eakins. "Anyway, we had all these animals, and then a pack of Nightkillers moved into the area. They started at our neighbor's farm, taking an animal almost every night. When he started sitting out at night waiting for them with his rifle, they moved to another farm about five miles up the road, and when that farmer started waiting for them, they went back to the first farm and grabbed another bull, just when he thought they'd gone away and his stock was safe.

"My dad, he didn't pay much attention to it until they started picking off our cattle one by one. There was no sense tracking them and trying to shoot them, because they could travel twenty miles before he could travel two. And there wasn't much sense in sitting out every night, because there were a lot of farms in the area, and they'd just go hunting where they couldn't smell no men and no guns."

Clark shifted his weight impatiently, but a quick look from Washington stopped him from saying anything.

"Well, my dad, he didn't want to sit up every night protecting the animals, because he had a farm to run and a family to head. He thought about what to do, and finally he came up with an idea, and he went to our five nearest neighbors and asked them if they'd each contribute a goat or a lamb, just one animal from each, and he promised that within a week all the Nightkillers would be dead.

"Now, Obidiah Nelson—he lived about four miles up the road—he said it wouldn't work, that Nightkillers could always spot poisoned bait and they wouldn't touch it, but Pap said he wasn't poisoning nothing, that he was going to teach the Nightkillers how to come out and get killed.

"No one knew what he was talking about, but after the Nightkillers hit two of their farms again they had a quick meeting, and that afternoon they came up the road with four goats and a lamb and left them with us. My dad said to come back in six nights and they could kill all the Nightkillers then."

"Sounds like magic," said one of the lieutenants contemptuously.

"That's what I thought too," said Eakins. "Didn't bother me none, though—I was real young and I believed in magic back then. Still do, on occasion—but it wasn't magic at all. It was just common sense.

"The first night Pap took one of the goats out into the far fields of our farm and cut its throat with a butcher knife. He left it there in a puddle of its own blood, and backed up maybe a hundred yards. Then he pulled a little whistle out of his pocket, kind of like the one Miss Blakely here was using, and he whistled a little melody on it, just three or four notes, and repeated it over and over. Pretty soon the wind shifted, and the Nightkillers could smell the blood, and right away they showed up at the goat's carcass and started eating. They could see my dad standing there, but he didn't bother them none nor try to get any closer, so they ignored him and just started gobbling the goat as fast as they could.

"Pap came back to the house and said he made it seven Nightkillers in the pack, but he could have missed one or two, and tomorrow night he'd leave a lantern near the next carcass, and that the lantern wouldn't bother the Nightkillers because it didn't smell like a man, and sure enough they didn't pay it any mind at all, and he came home and told us that there were eight of 'em.

"He killed a goat and a lamb the next two nights, and played his little melody, and each time the Nightkillers showed up sooner than the night before. On the fifth night he killed the goat before he took it out to the field, and didn't bleed it at all. He just played his three notes over and over, and they showed up maybe a minute later and started feeding on the goat.

"All the neighbors showed up on the sixth night, and Pap even let me and my three brothers take muskets out to the field. He stuck four lanterns around the place, so it was all lit up and you could see real well, and then he played his little melody, and sure enough, in less than a minute all eight Nightkillers were out there looking for their dinner, and in another minute we had eight dead Nightkillers, and from that day to this no Nightkillers ever bothered us again."

"Interesting," said Washington.

"I don't see what it has to do with Mrs. Blakely's Skyraiders," said one of the lieutenants.

Washington smiled. "Tell them, Mr. Eakins."

"My pap trained a pack of wild Nightkillers to come out and get themselves shot when they heard a whistle," said Eakins, "and he did it in only six nights. I don't see why we can't train a bunch of Skyraiders that are already tame and used to people to come when they hear a whistle. I could stay here for a week or two, until they learn that whenever they hear the whistle, if they come to it they're going to get fed.

"Now, Skyraiders got great eyes and ears, because they can see or hear a sick or dying animal from twenty or thirty miles away. I'll carve me a real high-pitched whistle, one they can hear over the winds, and get them to come to a different place every day, until I can call them from thirty or forty miles away, and once I know they'll come every time, I'll load a bunch of 'em onto one of Mrs. Blakely's wagons and come back to camp with 'em—or hunt up wherever the new camp is."

"We don't know yet that Mrs. Blakely is a willing partner," said Washington. He turned to the wiry woman. "What reimbursement will you want for your Skyraiders, their cages, and a wagon to transport them?"

"You just kill as many of the Redcoats as you can, General Washington," she replied. "Especially from the company that killed my husband. That'll be payment enough."

"Madam, you are a true patriot," said Washington. He turned to the young man. "Lieutenant Eakins," he said, "I want you to carve five or six whistles, not just one. And if you have the skill, I'd like you to give them a pitch or tone that's unusual and seldom heard. I don't want the British to be able to duplicate it if they figure out what we're doing."

"Yes, sir!" said Eakins, standing at attention and snapping off a crisp salute.

"Lieutenant Wilcox," said Washington, "I want you to remain with Lieutenant Eakins until I send some men down here to work with him. Although you have seniority, this is his project, and I hope you will make every effort to help him with as little friction as possible."

"Yes, sir," said Wilcox.

"And stop looking as if I just shot your best friend."

"Yes, sir," said Wilcox, trying not to look unhappy about his assignment and failing miserably.

"Mrs. Blakely," said Washington, "may my men have permission to sleep in your barn or one of the other outbuildings?"

"Certainly not," replied Amanda Blakely firmly. "They will sleep in the house, like human beings. My barns are for my dragons."

"Thank you very much, Mrs. Blakely," said Washington. "I'm sure they will appreciate it." He paused. "Do you mind if I ask you a question?"

"You don't need my permission to ask a question, General Washington," she replied. "You're the commander, and this is wartime."

"Thank you. My question is this: Surely you haven't domesticated all these Skyraiders merely so that an employee eighty miles away can send you messages about the operation of the farm. If he had a crisis that needed a quick decision, you couldn't get your reply back to him,

125

as the Skyraiders all come to you, not to him. So why have you been raising and working with them?"

"My husband left me three farms, but they don't make any money," said Amanda Blakely. "I needed to find a new source of income. I know it makes me sound like a ghoul, but I found that income on the battlefields that were strewn with the bodies of Americans and Redcoats. I first noticed it when I went to Saratoga to claim my husband's body. The rats had gotten there days earlier. There were seven, perhaps eight hundred bodies that had been chewed and gnawed beyond recognition. Everywhere we've engaged the British, we leave behind the dead and the dying—and the rats. And while some have argued against it, I believe that rats are also the carriers of disease.

"I'm too old and too slow to catch rats, but my Skyraiders aren't. I visit whatever municipality is in proximity of a battlefield, and I charge them to eradicate all the rats. The only trick was to make sure the dragons could be handled by my staff at the battlefield; they'd always fly back home to me after they'd killed every last rat they saw."

"Then why are they available to us, if I may be so bold as to ask?" said Washington. "It's fair to say that you won't be running out of battlefields anytime soon."

"We're at war, sir," she replied. "If my Skyraiders will help the war effort in even a small way, how can I refuse?"

"I wish all Americans thought as you do, Mrs. Blakely," said Washington. "I'll have the quartermaster send you payment for the use of your dragons. I think you'll find that freedom tastes even better if you're not destitute." He turned to face his men. "Are there any objections to trying Lieutenant Eakins's plan? If so, I want to hear them now, before I leave."

Silence.

"Good luck, Lieutenant Eakins. I'll expect you back in a week to ten days with a progress report." He paused. "And Lieutenant Bates, we'll put you in charge of the other half of the exercise."

"Sir?" said Bates, confused.

"I want you to take a crew of a dozen enlisted men, go to a few battlefields where Mrs. Blakely's Skyraiders have not yet been sent—I'm sure she can supply you with a list of names—and capture as many rats as you can. I should think the absolute minimum we'll want will be a hundred. Two hundred would be even better."

"Capture, sir—not kill?"

"That's right."

"And what do we do with these rats after we capture them?" asked Bates.

"Just feed them and keep them healthy," said Washington.

"I'll follow your orders, of course, sir," said the young officer. "But for the life of me I can't understand them. What am I missing, sir?"

"If we're successful in our use of the Skyraiders," said Washington, "you can be sure the British will follow suit. I want to have a hundred or more fat tasty rats ready to release. When a British letter carrier swoops down to grab a little lunch, we'll at least have a chance at shooting him and intercepting the message."

Clark smiled. For the first time in months, he thought that they might actually have a chance against the British.

CHAPTER FIFTEEN

Washington bent low over his desk, trying to better see the letter he was writing in the dim light. He could have put on his spectacles, but he didn't want the men to see him wearing them. He didn't consider them a sign of weakness, and they clearly improved his vision, but it could instill doubts in the men when he surveyed a battlefield and started issuing orders, and they had enough problems in this war without adding any uncertainty to their minds.

So he lowered his head still more, moved the lamp closer to the paper, and continued writing:

Dear Thomas:

I am writing to you as a fellow Virginian, because I cannot seem to make my needs clear to Hancock, Adams, and that bunch of Northeasterners who are in control of the Continental Congress. We are short of guns, ammunition, food, clothing, indeed just about everything. I cannot ask my men to go through another winter without shoes or overcoats. I have made request after request for supplies. Most of my entreaties have been ignored, and when they have been acted upon, the items that arrive are far less in quantity and far inferior in quality than I have asked for.

Our morale is surprisingly high, considering that no one in our embryonic government seems to want to send us the wherewithal to fight this damnable war, so I am asking you personally to do what you can. Right now my cannons are for show, for I have no cannonballs and no powder to fire them even if I had cannonballs. Furthermore, we have only one doctor to tend to our wounded, and since he himself had been shot in the leg . . .

Washington paused, looked at what he had written, grunted, and crumpled the missive into a ball.

I can't send that, he thought. *If he reads it, he'll tear up his Declaration and begin writing the terms of our surrender. We'll just have to make do, as we have been doing for the past two years.*

He pulled out the maps of the area, with the estimates of the British positions marked in red, and his own forces in blue. It looked like an even distribution of men, but he knew better. One side—the *wrong* side—had more than enough supplies, and his advance scouts reported that British reinforcements were on the way.

Finally he became too restless to continue working. He folded the map neatly, blew out the lamp, got to his feet, and walked out of his tent. The first man to see him called the others to attention.

"At ease, Corporal," said Washington. "I'm just taking a stroll and enjoying the evening breeze."

The men looked like they didn't believe him at first, but then one by one they broke their stance and went back to whatever they were doing, which consisted mostly of sitting around small campfires and conversing in low tones.

Suddenly there was a commotion from the direction of the nearby river, and a moment later four soldiers came up from the bank, proudly holding a dozen fish aloft.

"We eat real food tonight!" cried one of them.

"Get them pans ready!" said another.

"You boys have got to be crazy, going fishing in the dark," said a sergeant who was holding a mug of tea in his hand.

"They bite better at night," replied one of the fishermen.

"They're not the only things that bite," said the sergeant meaningfully.

"The Redcoats don't bite, they shoot," replied the man. "Besides, even the advance parties ain't within three miles of the river."

"I wasn't talking about the Redcoats," said the sergeant.

"There's dragons in them waters, big enough to swallow a boat whole."

"Oh, come on, Jim," said a fisherman. "You're talking about sea serpents out of fairy tales. You ain't never seen a dragon that lives in the water, nor one that could eat a boat. Those are just tales to scare kids with."

"No, sir," said Sergeant Jim firmly. "There's dragons, all right!"

"Jim, the damned river ain't eight feet deep. Where do you suppose these here dragons are hiding?"

"The rivers lead to lakes and oceans," persisted Jim. "And who's to say they don't go there to lie up after they've eaten their fill in the rivers. I heard it from Enoch Remson. He swears he seen one take a whole fishing vessel on Lake Erie, the boat and three men too. And Billy James says the river by his farm in Georgia is full of 'em."

"Enoch's a liar and Billy ain't drawn a sober breath all year."

"Anyone here ever seen a dragon that lives in the water?" asked one of the other fishermen. "Forget how big it has to be. Truth now—has anyone actually seen one?"

There was no response.

"You're asking the wrong question," said Washington, and suddenly all eyes turned to him.

"I beg your pardon, sir?" said the fisherman. "Just what question *should* I be asking?"

"How many of you have heard about sea dragons?" asked Washington.

About two-thirds of the men responded.

"And how many of you believe in them?"

The number didn't change appreciably.

"Thank you," said Washington, his face alive with excitement. Suddenly he was unable to stand still, and he began pacing around the camp, lost in thought. Finally he realized he was making the men nervous, and he retired to his tent.

George Rogers Clark entered a moment later. "I know that look, sir," he said. "You've got an idea."

"I do," Washington confirmed.

"Would you care to share it with me?"

"I have to work out the details."

"Perhaps I can help," said Clark.

Washington nodded his consent. "Did you hear what I asked the men?"

"No, but I heard *about* it."

"Did you know that two-thirds of them believe in sea dragons, dragons big enough to swallow a fishing boat whole?"

"What can I tell you?" said Clark. "We don't have the best-educated troops in the world."

"You're missing the point, George," said Washington. "These men were born here. They grew up in America. No one's ever seen a sea dragon, and to the best of my knowledge there aren't any, but two-thirds of the men believe that sea dragons—*huge* sea dragons—exist."

Clark frowned in puzzlement.

"If men who have lived here all their lives believe in them, why shouldn't the British, who never saw a dragon before they landed here, believe in the same thing?"

"Where is this leading, sir?" asked Clark.

"Let me tell you where it's *not* leading," said Washington. "It's not leading across the river!" Clark still looked mystified, and Washington continued. "I wouldn't anticipate our supplies arriving in less than a week. If the British cross the river before then, we don't stand a chance. So the trick is getting them to stay on their side of the river."

"And you're going to convince them there are boat-eating dragons in the river?" asked Clark, wondering whether or not Washington was pulling his leg.

"I'm going to try," responded Washington.

"How?"

"First we must have the blacksmith create some over-sized harpoons. We'll put them in the wreckage of a boat and arrange to have it strewn across the riverbank on the British side—and I want enormous teeth marks in that wreckage, as if something monumental bit it in half."

"You think one wrecked boat and a bunch of harpoons will convince them?" said Clark dubiously.

"No," admitted Washington. "But it's a start. Sacrifice one of our horses and make sure the wreckage is soaked with its blood. Next, let's not bury all our dead. Take three or four corpses, remove those portions of the bodies that bear bullet wounds, rip apart some of their limbs the way a sea monster might, and see to it that they aren't separated from the wrecked boat. Stick a letter in a corpse's pocket to the effect that I'm taking a terrible risk, crossing dragon-filled rivers, even hunting sea dragons for food, and the men think it's nothing short of suicidal. Then I want some of our Indians to take the totem of the Indians that are friendly to the British, cross the river a few miles upstream, and report our position to the British commander—and in the process, warn him that the river is infested with dragons, maybe tell him that they lost a few comrades while crossing it." Washington paused as his mind raced ahead, coming up with more notions. "How many meat animals have we got left?"

"I don't know, sir," said Clark. "Remember, my army only joined up with yours four days ago."

"I think it's four cattle and a sheep, but it could be five. Whatever it is, it should be enough."

"Enough for what?"

"I want to move the cattle toward the river. We can build a corral that the British advance column can see from their side. Then, each night at twilight, while they can still see, we'll tether one cow or steer to a post right by the water, as if it's an offering to the sea dragons, something for them to eat so they don't eat *us*. We'll very quietly move it after midnight, not to the corral, but inland a mile or more, so that each morning there will be one less animal, which should help convince them that the sea dragons took our offering—especially if we let a chewed up leg wash up on their side of the river."

"Sooner or later they'll figure out what you're doing," said Clark.

"Later is acceptable," said Washington. "It's sooner that I'm worried about. We've got to keep them on their side of the river until our ammunition arrives."

"I don't know . . ." said Clark.

"That's because you're an American. You've spent your whole life sharing the land with dragons, so you know what kind exist and what kind are fables. But put yourself in the shoes of the British. They'd heard about our dragons, of course, but they never saw one until the war began. Since then they've seen Skyraiders and Longgliders overhead, they've seen all the dozen sizes and varieties of Darters, they've lost meat animals and even some men to Nightkillers. So if we act as if there are monsters in this river, even though we crossed the Delaware and the Potomac with impunity, they have no reason not to believe us." Suddenly he smiled a very weak smile. "I hope."

Clark was silent for a long moment. Finally he spoke. "It's got possibilities."

"I hope so," said Washington. "When you don't have the firepower, you improvise. You cross the Delaware. You fight from ambush like the Indians. You live off the land. And," he concluded wryly, "you enlist imaginary dragons on your side."

"If this ruse is successful, I think you should add a pair of leathery wings to your family crest, sir," said Clark with a smile.

"First it has to work, then we'll worry about crests," replied Washington. "Pass the word to my officers, and yours as well. I want to see them all in ten minutes." He looked around. "They won't fit in any tent we have. I'll leave the meeting place up to you. Let me know when everyone is assembled."

Clark got to his feet, saluted, and left the tent.

A few minutes later he returned and informed Washington that they were gathered a short distance away. Washington emerged from his tent and approached the officers.

"Gentlemen," he said, "as most of you know, it would be disastrous if the British were to cross the river and attack us before our supplies and munitions arrive, and there is no reason to believe that they will be here in less than a week. The British are camped about forty miles away, and they have three advance parties posted within a few miles of us, on the far side of the river. Our job is to keep them there, and I have come up with what I admit is an audacious notion for accomplishing that end."

He spent the next few minutes explaining his idea, and the means he had already devised for bringing it to fruition. When he finished he looked around and concluded, "I'd like you to spend the night considering other ways we can convince the British that they dare not cross the river for fear of dragons, or at least that they will have to spend an enormous amount of time building boats and barges that can withstand the anticipated attacks. Feel free to discuss your ideas with each other. We will meet here after breakfast, at which time I will listen to your proposals and incorporate those that seem most promising of success. That is all, gentlemen. You are dismissed—and do try to get those stunned expressions off your faces before you come into contact with the troops."

The officers dispersed, and Washington began walking back to his tent, but his mind was too restless for him to sleep, and he continued walking around the camp, lost in thought. Hundreds of possibilities occurred to him; most he rejected, a few he filed away for further consideration.

Suddenly he realized that he had been walking along the river for the last few minutes. He glanced out at it, seeing the moonlight play over the ripples caused by the current.

"Wouldn't it be funny," he said with a wistful smile, "if it were true?"

CHAPTER SIXTEEN

The British didn't approach the river for nine days. As they drew closer, Washington's scouts reported back that the enemy had outrun their supply lines and were waiting to reestablish them. Also, they'd sustained more casualties in the last encounter than previously thought.

The sea dragon ruse was slowing them down. They camped two miles inland and sent their own scouts thirty miles along the river in each direction. Though no one reported back that any dragons had been spotted, the British commander was reluctant to commit his troops to a crossing, especially when each morning the animal that had been staked out the previous evening had disappeared.

It was exactly two weeks after Washington came up with the notion of sea dragons that Ephram Eakins returned to camp and stood at the entrance of his tent. After an exchange of greetings, the young lieutenant began his report.

"I brought twenty of them back with me, sir," said Eakins. "The rest took more training, and I left Lieutenant Wilcox behind to keep working with them." Suddenly he grinned. "Training the dragons was easy compared to teaching Lieutenant Wilcox to play a melody on the whistle." Washington smiled. Eakins continued. "I've taught them two simple melodies, sir. Each one has just four notes, so any of the men with a musical bent should be able to pick it up."

"*Two* melodies?"

"Yes, sir. One tells them to come to the person who's playing it, and one tells them to fly as high as they can and find someone else who's playing the same melody."

"We can't have one man play it continuously," said Washington. "What if they can't hear a melody when they're aloft?"

"They can glide on the thermals for hours, sir. As long as the person who's summoning them plays for a few minutes every three or four hours, they'll be able to find him."

"How is their night vision?"

"They do most of their hunting by day, but they can see at night. Not as well, but well enough—and they'll be following their ears. They won't need to see who's playing until they're ready to land."

"What's their limit? How far away can they be before we can't count on them hearing the melody that summons them?"

"I don't know, sir."

"Didn't Amanda Blakely say something about eighty miles?" asked Washington.

"Yes, sir," replied Eakins. "But those were Skyraiders that were released eighty miles from the spot they were born. I would guess that they could fly five hundred miles and get to that spot with no trouble. But I don't know how far they can go before they can't hear the melody at the other end."

"So if a Skyraider can't hear the melody, is he likely to fly back to Mrs. Blakely's farm?"

"It's possible, sir. But they can surely hear it from eight or ten miles, and once they're a little better trained and know they're looking for whoever's playing the melody, they can probably double or triple that distance. At that point, even if they can't hear it, they'll know to circle around until they do hear it."

"Ten miles," repeated Washington. "I had hoped for more range. Still, the British are within four miles, so for the moment that range should be sufficient."

Eakins reached into his pocket and withdrew a handful of whistles, which he placed on Washington's desk. "Here, sir—a gift from Mrs. Blakely. She carved them while Lieutenant Wilcox and I were working with the Skyraiders."

"That woman is a treasure," said Washington. "I must remember to write and thank her."

"I'm sure she'll appreciate it, sir," said Eakins. "I don't want to sound blasphemous, but she practically worships you."

"Her prayers would be better directed toward the Almighty," said Washington. "I'm just a soldier, doing my best to help an infant country become free of its parent."

There was an awkward silence.

"Well, sir," said Eakins at last, "I'd better get some help unloading the crates and doing what I can to make the Skyraiders comfortable."

"Take as many men as you think you'll need," said Washington. Eakins saluted and turned to leave the tent. "Just a minute, Lieutenant!"

"Yes, sir?" said Eakins, turning and facing Washington.

"What are you feeding the Skyraiders?"

"We butchered a cow yesterday, and I've been tossing scraps of meat into their cages," answered Eakins. "They can eat carrion, so it won't be too high for them for another few days. Then I suppose we'll feed them some of the rats Lieutenant Bates was supposed to find for you."

Washington shook his head. "No we won't."

"Sir?" said Eakins, puzzled.

"We've got to find out if they'll behave as expected before we have to depend on them," said Washington. "So first thing tomorrow morning, I want you to let three or four Skyraiders loose. Let them take off and go hunting for food. If they swoop down and make a kill, or find some carrion, let them eat—but the minute they start approaching the limit of your whistle's range, I want you to play your melody and see if they respond to it in strange surroundings."

"And if they don't?"

"Then you'll take the rest back to Mrs. Blakely's farm for more schooling," said Washington. "I can't use them if I can't rely on them."

"All right, sir. I'll turn them loose at sunup." He saluted and left the tent.

Messenger dragons, imaginary dragons—it's a hell of a way to fight a war, thought Washington. *Maybe my friend Daniel can scare up some British-eating dragons out West. But in the meantime . . .*

He fell to studying his maps again. If the attack came before his supplies arrived, he could fall back here, split his forces there, position snipers on this ridge, set a brushfire along the northern edge of that field. He'd been fighting this kind of battle for years now. It wasn't what he'd trained for, and it wasn't what he had in mind when he joined the army. Someday he'd like to meet the British with an equal force, fully equipped and properly trained.

Finally he shook his head. It wasn't going to happen, not in this lifetime—so he'd make do with what he had, and if that meant making use of real Skyraiders and mythical sea dragons, it was better than *not* having them in his arsenal. Still, it was a hell of a way to fight a war. . . .

He heard a cough and sat up abruptly. It was daylight, and he realized he'd fallen asleep at his desk, as he had done more and more often these past few months.

"Sir?" said Lieutenant Bates gently.

Washington blinked his eyes, and when they still wouldn't focus, he rubbed them, then stared at Bates again. This time he saw what he was supposed to see.

"Yes, Lieutenant?"

"I'm sorry to wake you, sir, but I'm afraid we have a situation that requires a command decision."

"The British?" asked Washington, instantly alert.

"No, sir," said Bates. "The rats."

"I beg your pardon?"

"The rats, sir. We've got about three hundred of them penned up, as you ordered."

"I know."

"Well, Mr. Eakins let three of his Skyraiders loose this morning. I gather it was something of an experiment, to see if they would return after they'd flown a few miles away."

Washington nodded his head. "Go on."

"Well, they won't fly away, sir," said Bates. "The second he let them loose, they raced over to the pen where we're keeping the rats, and they're doing their damnedest to tear it apart."

"Damn!" said Washington. "I should have thought of that."

"So we need a decision, sir," continued Bates. "Do we turn some rats loose for them, or do we gather them up and put them back in their cages?"

"Put them back in their cages, and send Lieutenant Eakins to me."

Bates saluted and left, and Eakins arrived less than a minute later.

"I hear we have a problem, Lieutenant," said Washington.

"Yes, sir," replied the young man. "I never thought of it, but of course they can see and hear the rats, and probably smell them too, and they don't feel the need to go any farther in search of food."

"I want you to take the dragons two miles inland from the river. How long will that take you?"

"Maybe half an hour, sir."

"We'll let five or six of the rats loose behind the camp in forty minutes. If they make a kill along the way, fine. If not, and they kill the rats here, I want you to summon them back with your melody, and let's see if they respond."

"I don't think they will, sir," said Eakins.

"You assured me that they were trained," said Washington, frowning.

"They are, sir," replied Eakins. "But they know you've got hundreds of rats penned up here. If they kill some, it might be very difficult to get them to leave when they know the rest are still here. It might work better if Lieutenant Bates were to set some loose a few miles to the south and west."

"No," said Washington, as the solution suddenly became clear to him. "We don't have to worry about their flying back to Amanda Blakely's farm when they're out of earshot. All we have to do is teach them to know that every time they return here from wherever they've been taken, there will be a meal for them."

"I suppose that'll work, sir," agreed Eakins. "But how will we convince them to carry a message *from* here to our men in the field?"

"Probably we won't, at least not for a while," said Washington. "But Ben Franklin has a saying, that half a loaf is better than none. It's more important that I *know* they'll bring messages to us from the field than that I *hope* they'll carry messages in both directions. There are enough uncertainties in war without knowingly adding to them."

"All right, sir," said Eakins. "I'll have some of them moved a mile or two away and turned loose, and as soon as they're overhead we'll turn a few rats loose." He paused. "And I'll also play on the whistle, just to be on the safe side."

"Take them in groups of six and seven, so that we only have to make three trips a day to teach all twenty of them."

Eakins saluted and left the tent.

Washington stood up, stretched his stiff muscles, yawned once, and began walking around the tent, pounding his feet on the floor in an attempt to bring a little life to them.

Cornwallis makes decisions regarding the disposition of his troops, he thought. *Lord Rawdon probes our weak spots and attacks only when the numbers are right. And what kind of command decisions do I make? What to do with the rats.*

Suddenly Washington chuckled. *Who knows? Maybe such innovation is the stuff that victories are made of.*

He had his doubts, but on a beautiful morning like this he chose to ignore them.

CHAPTER SEVENTEEN

Four days later, in late afternoon, Eakins reported that the Skyraiders had proven responsive, and could probably be counted on to return to camp whenever they were released.

"*Probably?*" repeated Washington.

"We won't know until we release them in battle conditions, sir," said Eakins. "We know they'll fly thirty miles back to camp, because I measured the distance—but we don't know for sure that they'll do it if they're being shot at, or if there are bodies littering the ground. Rats aren't the only scavengers; Skyraiders will eat dead flesh as quick as any other animal."

"I understand your concerns about the bodies," said Washington, "but we've never used Skyraiders in war before. Why should they be fired upon?"

"When soldiers on either side outrun their supply lines, they'll shoot at just about anything they can eat," answered Eakins.

I'm out of practice keeping such considerations in mind,
thought Washington sardonically. *I haven't seen a supply
line in close to two years.*

"Well, Lieutenant Eakins, we'd better put them to the
test while they can still prove useful. I want you and five
men of your choosing to take a Skyraider in its cage, raft
across the river about fifteen miles upstream, and start
scouting the enemy positions. One man will do the
scouting, one will stay with the Skyraider and keep it
calm. When you learn anything of use, attach the message to the Skyraider and turn it loose."

"Then what, sir?"

"Then make your way back to camp as circuitously
and carefully as you can," said Washington. "If the battle
hasn't started yet, you can go back across the river with
another Skyraider and gather more information. If we've
had to move, you're a good enough tracker to find us. I
suggest you choose men who are equally good."

"Too bad Dan'l Boone ain't here, sir," said Eakins. "I
know he's a friend of yours, and from what I hear tell, he
could track a billiard ball down the paved streets of
Boston." He paused. "Is there any reason *why* he ain't in
uniform, sir? We could sure use someone like him."

"I hope he'll be joining us before long," replied Washington. "He's on a mission for me."

"I *knew* it!" said Eakins. "Some of the men were saying
he didn't have any interest in fighting the British, but I
knew it wasn't so!"

Washington smiled gently at the younger man.
"Lieutenant, if this mission is as successful as some of
his others, it may prove more important than having
one more officer, even such a gifted one, under my
command."

"Are those stories they tell about him really true?"
asked Eakins.

"I don't know which stories you're referring to, but they probably are," replied Washington. "Or mostly true, anyway. We'll talk about him some other time. Right now you have a job to do, do you not?"

"Yes, sir," said Eakins, snapping to attention and saluting. "Right away, sir."

He hastened off to round up five men and choose the Skyraiders he needed, and Washington began walking through the camp. He felt it was essential that his men see him every day, that he exude confidence no matter what he felt, that he listen to their complaints and their suggestions, and he hoped that by doing this he wouldn't have to listen to their fears because his presence and attitude would help dissipate any fears they had.

"Good afternoon, General," said one of the men minding a cannon that was aimed across the river.

"Good afternoon," replied Washington. "Anything interesting happening on the other side?"

"I think we've got 'em scared half to death, sir," said the man. "All day long they've been bringing lumber up to within about half a mile, right behind that rise there. You can't see 'em from here, but I've seen them carrying it from a couple of miles away." He grinned. "I'll bet they're figuring on making a bunch of dragonproof barges, sir, and ferrying their men across the river."

"Based on what you've seen, have you any idea how soon it might be ready?" asked Washington.

"Beats me, sir. I don't know how many men it has to carry. Figures to be pretty big, though. They have to know if they just land twenty or thirty men at a time, we'll pick 'em off like sitting ducks."

"And how long have they been bringing the lumber to the river?"

"Just started this morning, sir."

"So even if they've got half their men chopping down trees and turning them into boards, we probably have a few days?" asked Washington, as a plan started taking shape.

The soldier nodded his agreement. "I can't imagine they could do it much sooner, sir."

"Thank you, Sergeant," said Washington. He called an aide over and told him to find Eakins before he left with the Skyraiders. The young Pennsylvanian approached him a few minutes later.

"You sent for me, sir?" he said.

"Yes, Lieutenant," said Washington. "When you get across the river, what I want you to concentrate on is not the disposition of the troops who are presumably building the barges, or indeed any of the force that we expect to attack us. I want you to go inland at least twenty miles and let me know if there are any British reinforcements on the way."

"But the ones just across the river are the ones we have to worry about, sir," protested Eakins.

"I'll do the worrying, Lieutenant," said Washington. "You just follow your orders."

"Yes, sir," said Eakins, looking at him as if he'd gone temporarily mad. He even forgot to salute, and Washington decided not to mention the lapse.

Eakins and his men and Skyraiders left two hours later, right after twilight, and Washington had nothing to do now but wait. He decided not to share his plan with his men yet, not that he felt any of them would go over to the British and reveal it to them, but rather because he knew they were under constant observation by British spyglasses and he wanted them to act as natural as possible.

In the morning he sent Lieutenant Bates and a squad of six men to Amanda Blakely's farm, with orders to evacuate Mrs. Blakely and her remaining Skyraiders and take them to her most distant farm, eighty miles farther away.

Washington spent the next two days waiting impatiently for the information he needed. Just before daybreak of the third day, a Skyraider swooped down and landed right next to the pen that held all the rats. One of the men immediately approached him, detached the pouch from his leg, released a couple of rats, and took the pouch to Washington as the Skyraider emitted a hiss of glee and made short and grisly work of the two unfortunate rodents.

Washington pulled the folded paper out of the pouch and read it.

Mr. General Washington, sir,

There ain't no British within twenty mile of the force what's gathered acrost the river from you. In fact, there ain't none more than five mile away.

Corporal William Lawson

"Warm up a meal for Corporal Lawson and his partner," said Washington to an aide, folding the paper and putting it in a pocket. "I imagine they'll be back in camp by noon, and they probably haven't seen much more than jerky and berries for three days now."

The aide saluted and left.

So far so good, thought Washington.

Late that evening a second Skyraider returned, bearing a similar message. The following morning a third Skyraider came back with a note from Eakins, who'd chosen to roam far to the west rather than cover the same ground as his companions, and hadn't seen any sign of the British.

Washington summoned Lieutenant Wilcox, and the officer arrived a few minutes later.

"You sent for me, sir?" he asked.

Washington nodded. "I need to know the exact strength of the British force across the river. This will be a very dangerous assignment, because it's pretty open territory, and you won't be able to get the information I need under cover of darkness. Cross about ten miles upstream or downstream, and take a Skyraider and another man to tend it. Once you have what I need, attach the message to the Skyraider and the two of you make your way back as carefully as possible. If you feel it's too dangerous, just stay there; the British will be crossing the river soon."

"Yes, sir," said Wilcox, saluting and heading off to find a partner and a Skyraider.

Eakins made it back to camp in midafternoon. After he had eaten, Washington sent for him.

"You did a fine job, Captain Eakins," he said. "As soon as I know the British are ready to attack us, I have another one for you."

"Captain?" the young man repeated reverently.

"Captain," confirmed Washington. "Now pay attention to the task at hand."

"Yes, sir!" said Eakins happily.

"You will take one hundred men and head due west. I want you to do everything you can to make it look like you have three thousand men with you. Build twenty fires for every one you use, leave hundreds of holes for tent poles even though you set up no tents, and do whatever is possible to convince anyone following you that you're an army in retreat. Can I count on you to do that?"

"For how long, sir?"

"I'm not sure yet," said Washington. "I'll let you know sometime tonight. Stay close by." Eakins saluted and turned to leave. "And Ephram . . ."

"Sir?"

"Don't get too far ahead of them. I don't want them getting discouraged, or thinking that it's a ruse. Send scouts out, and make sure you're being pursued. If they've stopped or turned back, have the scouts fire a few shots at them and then retreat instantly."

"Then what, sir?" asked Eakins. "We can't hold the British off with one hundred men."

"You won't have to," said Washington. "I can't tell you anything further right now. I'm still working out the details. But I'll get back to you when the plan is complete."

The next afternoon Wilcox's Skyraider flew back to camp.

General Washington:

I make it almost five thousand regulars, and upwards of sixty cannons. It looks like they'll have the barges done in another two days. I think they plan to roll it to the river over a carpet of felled tree trunks.

Lieutenant James Wilcox

Another two days. And he'd written it last night. That meant this was the first day, and they'd be ready to cross tomorrow.

Washington sent for his three Mohawk Indians.

"The British are going to cross the river tomorrow in a number of barges made of wood," he said. "They will almost be floating forts."

"And you want us to fire flaming arrows into them?" suggested one of the Mohawks.

Washington shook his head. "They'll be on the water, and it would be very easy to put out a fire under those conditions. No, I want you to wait in hiding until after they all land. They may make ten or twenty trips on each barge to get all their men on this side of the river, but

151

eventually they'll get it done." He paused. *I'd better be right about this next part.* "Before the day is over they will have marched away. At that time, and no earlier, I want you to set fire to the barges. Then, when you are done, cross the river."

The Mohawk gave his version of a salute, and the three Indians left.

Well, he thought, *our mystical sea serpents bought us more than a week, and our Skyraiders have provided me with the information I need. Now it's time to see if I've used that time and information properly, and God have mercy on the men who trust and follow me if I have not.*

CHAPTER EIGHTEEN

Washington called a meeting of his officers at twilight.

"Gentlemen," he said, "according to the best information we have, the British will complete their barges tomorrow. I think we can count on their crossing the river tomorrow afternoon, or the following morning at the very latest."

"We'll be ready for them, sir," said a major.

"They far outnumber us," said Washington. "Our job is to avoid battle and stay alive until we can join up with Daniel Morgan's forces, which I understand are some four hundred miles south and east of us, or possibly Nathanael Greene's regiment, which is on the move down in the Carolinas. It would be foolhardy to meet the British head-on with what we've got."

"I don't mean to be impertinent, sir," said a captain, "but if we never intended to fight them, what have we been doing, staying here for weeks while they gathered their forces and built their barges?"

"It's not an impertinent question at all, but a very legitimate one," answered Washington. "At first we were waiting for supplies and reinforcements, but it was obvious two weeks ago that neither were going to arrive. Then it became a question of how to negate all that British firepower without having to confront it. I think we're very close to accomplishing it, and we should complete the job in the next two days."

The officers, even more alert now, gathered closer, waiting to hear what their commander had to say.

"It will be dark in another hour. I want you each to pass the word down the chain of command that four hours from now we will evacuate the camp. I want it done with absolute silence. Those of you who have horses, wrap their feet to muffle the sound. At midnight you, Major Morris, will lead the march to the east, a mile inland from the river—and we will all march in single file. This is to be a covert evacuation, and it must be done by morning. When the sun comes up, I want us to be at least five miles east of here, and one mile inland from the river."

"They can read signs as well as we can, sir," said another officer. "Why won't they just follow us?"

"Because Captain Eakins, here, will be leaving a clear and unmistakable trail to the west." He turned to Eakins. "Have you selected your hundred men?"

"Yes, sir," said Eakins. "They're ready, and just awaiting your orders."

"You can start as soon as it's dark. Make as much noise as you like. They won't come across the river without their barges, and they won't be able to see well enough to shoot."

Eakins nodded. "Yes, sir."

"If all of us together can't hold the British off," said an officer, "how do you expect Eakins to do so with only one hundred men?"

"I don't."

"Is it really necessary to sacrifice them, sir?" persisted the officer.

"I'm not sacrificing anyone," said Washington. "At least, I hope I'm not. And if they come with us, the British will follow the only trail available to them and that is precisely the confrontation I am trying to avoid until we're stronger."

"Then I don't understand, sir."

"Captain Eakins," said Washington, turning back to the young man, "you will continue to march along the river, heading due west, for as long as your scouts tell you that the bulk of the British are following on your trail. One of two things will happen before a week has passed: Either they'll get too close, and confrontation will seem inevitable, or they will realize that they've been duped, and will retrace their steps and try to pick up our trail. I wouldn't anticipate either happening for at least three or four days, hopefully a little longer. But when one or the other transpires, swim across the river with your men before they can see what you've done."

"They'll follow our tracks to the water, sir," said Eakins. "It's going to be pretty hard to hide the fact that we crossed the river."

"We're not trying to hide it," explained Washington. "We just don't want them to know that everyone made it safely across. Remember, they think there are huge dragons in the river. Take along some extra clothes. At nights, when you've nothing else to do, shred the clothes. Then, when you swim the river, toss them in. When the clothes wash up on shore, the British will be convinced that a huge number of your men didn't make it across, and they won't cross back over until they've spent another week building more barges."

Washington paused long enough for his officers to comprehend his strategy, then continued. "We will march forty miles to the east, and then we too will cross the river, leaving the British on this side. If their supply line comes within hailing distance of the river, we'll destroy it. They'll be on the wrong side of the river, their barges will be destroyed, and while a small group of men can live off the land with no difficulty, I think it will be harder for four thousand men in a strange land to do the same. If they go south, they'll find Amanda Blakely's farm deserted. By the time they cross the river again, we'll have joined up with either Morgan or Greene, and then we'll be more than happy to meet them in combat."

"It still feels like running," muttered a junior officer.

His companions tried to hush him up, but Washington intervened.

"Son," he said, addressing him without mentioning his rank, "I've been striking and running for four years. If we'd had more time to prepare, to get our factories working, to build more roads and recruit more men, I would have preferred never to run. I am a general, and generals are trained to meet the enemy on the battlefield. But my job is to win the war, not puff out my chest and show how brave I am." He stared at the young man. "Military cemeteries the world over are filled with the graves of brave men. It's the smart ones who live long enough to win."

"I'm sorry, sir," said the junior officer. "I spoke without thinking."

"I admire your courage," said Washington. "But when you are outgunned and outnumbered, courage has to be tempered with judgment and intelligence. And now, gentlemen, if there are no questions, I think you'd best begin passing the word through the ranks."

"I have a question, sir," said Eakins. "What do we do with the Skyraiders?"

"Ah, yes, the Skyraiders," said Washington. "I'd forgotten about them. We can't take them with us; the cages,
and the wagon that pulls the cages, are too bulky. I
wouldn't want someone following our trail rather than
Captain Eakins's, at least not right away." He lowered his
head in thought for a moment. "Whether we keep them
caged or release them, they're not going away, not as
long as the rats remain here. I suppose if we turn the rats
loose, the subsequent commotion caused by the
Skyraiders might be enough to motivate the British to
leave the area at once and follow the trail Captain Eakins
is leaving for them." He considered the problem further,
then nodded his head decisively. "Yes, that's what we'll
do. Major Claiborne, take half a dozen men just before
we leave and let the Skyraiders out of their cages—but
not before you remove the pouches from their legs, and
any other accoutrements that would let the British de-
duce that they are domesticated. The Mohawks are staying behind to destroy the barges once the British go after
Captain Eakins, and will then join up with us on the
other side once we've made the crossing. Tell them to
wait until the first party of British is halfway across the
river and then let all the rats loose. No sense doing it
now, or they might be spread over too wide an area by
the time the British arrive."

Washington stopped and looked around. "Are there
any more questions? No? Good. Then let's pass the word
and start getting prepared. Anything bulky or noisy gets
left behind. If it's edible and it can't be carried, burn it or
bury it, but don't leave it for the enemy."

The officers dispersed, and Washington strolled over
to the river, staring across it in the fading light.

I've delayed you for two weeks, he thought, *and I've
stopped you from killing anyone during that time. It won't go
down in the history books as a triumph, but anything that buys*

us time and lets us live is a triumph just the same. I just wish we had something, anything, to match your weaponry.

And, more than a thousand miles to the west, three men were wondering if they had stumbled onto the weapon of Washington's dreams—and also wondering if they would survive their first glimpse of it.

PART THREE

POMPEY'S BOOK

CHAPTER NINETEEN

Pompey looked at the Thunderflame, trying to estimate how big it was. It was hopeless. The creature was so massive, so far beyond any known reference point, that he couldn't even be sure how far away it was.

"You ever see anything like that?" asked Boone.

"I'd have remembered," replied Pompey, resisting the urge to laugh. "My mother grew up in Africa. When I was a child she told me about elephants. I've never seen one, of course, but she drew pictures of them and described them to me. Until a minute ago I'd have bet they were the largest beasts in the world. But *this* Thunderflame"—Pompey shook his head in wonderment—"he makes up about five elephants."

"This is the dragon I have heard of all my life," said Gray Eagle with satisfaction. "This is the dragon I have come so far to find."

"What do they eat, I wonder?" asked Pompey nervously.

"They don't eat meat," said Tall Mountain. "We can approach him if you wish."

"Approach *that*?" said Pompey.

Tall Mountain smiled. "He will not harm you. I have already told you he does not eat meat." As if to emphasize the point, the Thunderflame began browsing on the leaves of a tree some twenty-five feet above the ground.

"He weighs a million pounds and with a name like Thunderflame, he can probably set us on fire from where he is," said Pompey.

"He will not harm you," repeated Tall Mountain. "Look at him. He has no fear. Everything else is hunted by something, but nothing hunts the Thunderflame. You can stand right next to him and he will ignore you."

"You do it first," said Pompey, unconvinced.

"We'll *all* do it," said Boone decisively, urging his Blue Nimble forward. The animal showed no fear; either it had approached Thunderflames before, or it sensed that the huge beast was not a predator. Banshee, too, seemed unconcerned, and remained on Boone's shoulder. "If this is the critter that's going to help Washington win the war, the sooner we figure out how to control it the better."

"I agree," said Gray Eagle. "There is a difference between approaching it and controlling it. We certainly can't control it from here."

Pompey reluctantly urged his mount forward, and the four men were soon within thirty yards of the Thunderflame. There they stopped and studied it in detail.

The creature stood fully fifteen feet at the shoulder, and was a deep, rich green in color, with a lighter green underbelly. It had a long, muscular neck that enabled it to reach succulent leaves and fruits thirty feet above the ground. Its head was in the same proportions as a horse's, but it had a number of bony protrusions along the cheekbones, the eye sockets were raised a few inches above the plane of the head, the ears were surprisingly small for a beast of that size, and the nostrils were quite large. It was as if Nature had decided that since nothing could kill it, it didn't need acute hearing or excellent vision, but it needed an exceptional sense of smell in its constant quest to fill its belly. The teeth were as numerous as the Cavedancer's or the Nightkiller's, but they were blunt, made for grinding rather than slashing.

The legs were the width of large tree trunks, but they ended in claws rather than hooves. The claws, some fifteen inches long, weren't especially sharp. Clearly they weren't made for rending the flesh of animals, but rather for gaining purchase on difficult terrains.

The tail was whiplike in proportion to the rest of the dragon, but given its size it seemed more like a twisted log some twenty feet long. Pompey couldn't see it being used as a rudder, and since nothing hunted Thunderflames, it probably wasn't a defensive weapon, whiplike or not.

There was a huge protrusion on each side of the dragon's rib cage, and Pompey asked Tall Mountain about it.

"They are born with wings," explained the Kiowa, "and the infants can actually fly for almost a year. Then they get too large and too heavy, and before long the wings fall off. What you see is what's left."

"How come the prairie isn't littered with Thunderflame wings, then?" asked Pompey.

"I said nothing eats the Thunderflame. What I meant was nothing *hunts* the adult Thunderflame. Packs of Nightkillers will feed on their abandoned wings, or feed on dead Thunderflames—or, if they feel they can avoid the mothers, prey on infant Thunderflames."

"How numerous are they?" asked Boone.

The Kiowa shrugged. "I have never seen many; their numbers are certainly not like the buffalo. The young usually stays with the mother for ten or twelve years, so they do not produce very many babies."

"Do they travel in packs, family units, or alone like this fellow here?" continued Boone.

"I have sometimes seen them in groups of fifteen or twenty," answered Tall Mountain. "Usually mothers and young. The males usually live alone."

"Are the females the same color?" asked Gray Eagle.

"They are a lighter green," said Tall Mountain. "The babies are yellow when they hatch out, and darken to green over the next ten to fifteen years." He paused. "Are you ready to approach him?"

"We *have* approached him," said Pompey.

"You can walk right up to him and touch him, as long as he sees you and you don't startle him."

"He probably wouldn't even feel a musket ball," remarked Boone.

"If he's this big, his skin probably can't be pierced by anything smaller than a cannonball, and nothing hunts him," said Pompey, "why is he a Thunderflame?"

"That is his name," said Tall Mountain.

"I assume that he can shoot a flame out of his mouth, like the Landwagons can?"

"Yes."

"Why?" persisted Pompey. "What does something like that need it for?"

"To protect his young."

Gray Eagle had dismounted. Handing his Blue Nimble's reins to Tall Mountain, he walked boldly up to the Thunderflame, which gave him a single glance and paid him no further attention. He strode over to a massive foreleg, pressed against it gently, and then—tensing, as if ready to duck and then roll beneath the creature's belly if he had to—he gave the leg a resounding slap. The Thunderflame didn't even notice it.

Encouraged by what he had seen, Pompey climbed down off his Blue Nimble and, like Gray Eagle, handed the reins to Tall Mountain. He made a little semicircle and approached from the left side. One of the Thunderflame's wide-set eyes swiveled and followed him for a moment, then looked ahead to the tree where it was eating.

Pompey walked beneath the dragon, and when he came out the other side, he reached up, grabbed the remnants of the right wing with both hands, and hung on it, bending his knees and swinging his feet off the ground. As with Gray Eagle's slap, the dragon seemed not to notice it at all.

Feeling safer, Pompey walked to the front of the dragon and looked up some twenty-five feet to where it was munching on huge mouthfuls of leaves.

"Hey, dragon!" he shouted.

The dragon flicked one ear, but otherwise paid him no attention.

It's like we're in two different universes, thought Pompey. *His is too big to even notice something as small as me.*

"Stand back," said Boone in Shawnee, and both Pompey and Gray Eagle immediately walked away from the dragon.

Boone waited until they were some twenty yards distant, then fired his rifle into the air.

The Thunderflame stopped eating, extended its long neck in Boone's direction, and stared at him curiously. A moment later it went back to its supper.

Pompey and Gray Eagle rejoined Boone and Tall Mountain a moment later.

"He seems docile enough," said Pompey. "The trick is how to get him mad at the British."

"There's a bigger problem than that," said Boone.

"Oh? What is it?"

"Let's see you make him move ten yards from where he's standing right now."

Pompey frowned. "Can we offer him food?"

"It'd take more than we can carry to tempt him when he's already eating," said Boone. "But let's say he's denuded the tree and is looking for something else. You offer him a few hundred pounds of whatever it is that he likes. He comes over and eats it. Now what? You can't do that every ten or fifteen yards, all the way back to a battlefield a thousand miles away."

"Maybe we could put it in a wagon, hook it up to some Blue Nimbles, and have them pull it just out of his reach," suggested Pompey.

"To New Jersey or the Carolinas?"

"Well, for a few miles at a time, to start with."

Boone shook his head. "Get him annoyed and all he'll do is burn you *and* his dinner."

"So it's a twofold problem," said Pompey. "First, how to move him, and second, once we've solved that, how to motivate him to attack the British."

"That's part of the problem, anyway," agreed Boone.

"There's more?"

"You yourself raised the question a while back: How do we teach him the difference between the Americans and the Redcoats?"

"Ah, yes. I recall," said Pompey with a frown.

An hour later, none of them had come up with an answer.

CHAPTER TWENTY

They camped in a mountain meadow surrounded by trees. The Thunderflame showed no fear when they built a fire at night, but kept moving from one bush or tree to the next, eating constantly. Tall Mountain insisted on standing guard against Nightkillers out beyond the circle of light. At first Boone said that he was inclined to talk him out of it; then he remembered that they were riding Blue Nimbles, not Landwagons, and that Nightkillers, even a large pack of them, were probably too insignificant a threat for the Thunderflame to take any notice of them—or any action against them.

"Doesn't he ever stop eating long enough to sleep?" asked Pompey, as the gigantic dragon began defoliating yet another tree.

"If you had to feed a body like that, would you?" responded Boone.

"Too bad we don't have a nice lady Thunderflame with us," said Pompey wistfully. "We could just walk her east and he'd follow us."

"Sometimes I wonder about you," said Boone dryly. "I really do."

"What's wrong with wishing we had a lady dragon?"

"First, if he was interested in the ladies, he'd be *there*. He wouldn't be all alone out here. I have to figure that any dragon that prefers our company to that of a lady dragon doesn't have much of a romantic nature."

"I never thought of that," admitted Pompey.

"There's also the obvious."

"Which is?"

"Pretend you've got your lady Thunderflame right here," said Boone, absently stroking Banshee as the little dragon wriggled with pleasure. "Pretend our gentleman Thunderflame is madly in love with her. Nothing's changed—except that you don't want to stand between them. You've still got the same problem: how are you going to make either one of them move ten yards? You say he'll follow her to the battlefield? All right, maybe he will. How do you get *her* there?"

"Surely you're not giving up on the very day we find the damned dragon, are you?" said Pompey.

"Of course not—but I can't waste my time with daydreams and fantasies. Finding a dragon that's powerful enough to turn the tide of battle is one thing. Transporting him is another. Teaching him who to do battle with is a third. And if we get that far, calling him off will be a fourth. All we've accomplished so far is the easy part of our job."

"Are you two going to speak in the language of the Long Knives all night?" demanded Gray Eagle irritably.

"I'm sorry," said Boone in Shawnee. "I hadn't realized we were." He paused. "Have you got any ideas about how to control the Thunderflame?"

"Food and females," answered Gray Eagle. "It is how you control every male of every species, including ours."

"I have a feeling that the females come into heat, like most other animals," said Boone.

"Why would you think that?" asked Pompey.

"There are no marks, no scars, no wounds of any kind on him," said Boone. "If he was driven away by a bigger, tougher male, he'd shown signs of it. And since he doesn't, it means he's here of his own choosing. Now, that could mean a lot of things, but it probably means no nearby females are in heat. If they could be bred year 'round, or if one of them was in heat right now, he wouldn't be here."

"There is another possibility," suggested Gray Eagle.

"Oh?" said Boone. "And what is that?"

"He is guarding a clutch of eggs while the female is off feeding."

Boone shook his head. "There's no spoor of a second Thunderflame anywhere near here. That means there are no eggs near here, and if this one was guarding any eggs, he'd never graze this far from them."

Gray Eagle considered Boone's answer, then nodded. "There are no females in heat," he said. To Pompey it sounded like a judge uttering a pronouncement.

"Now that we've settled that, how do we get him to move?" asked Boone. "And once we've figured that out, how do we get ten or twenty of his brothers to move along with him?"

"We wait for a female to come into heat," said Gray Eagle.

"Even Pompey can tell you what's wrong with that," said Boone.

Gray Eagle looked annoyed, and turned to Pompey to see what he had to say.

"How do you get the female to move to the battlefield?" offered Pompey.

All three men fell silent, each considering the problem, each hoping one of the other two would come up with a solution.

Finally Gray Eagle spoke up. "Perhaps Tall Mountain knows how to move a Thunderflame."

The other two exchanged looks.

"I already spoke to him, while you were building the fire. Pompey translated," replied Boone. "He can't imagine why anyone would *want* to make a Thunderflame move from one place to another. I even told him to imagine that a Thunderflame was walking through the Kiowa's fields, destroying their crops, and asked how they would get him to leave." Suddenly Boone smiled. "You know what he told me?"

"What?"

"That was why the Kiowa were hunters rather than farmers."

"Some help!" snorted Pompey.

"Anyway, it's why I haven't called him over," said Boone. He yawned and stretched his arms. "I suppose it's getting near time to get my bedroll and spread it out." He paused. "I mean no offense, but I'm getting mighty sick of your two faces being the last ones I see at night and the first ones in the morning. I've got a wife and six children, you know."

"I thought you had seven," said Pompey.

"I did," said Boone in tones that did not invite further questioning.

"You have only one wife?" said Gray Eagle, obviously amused by the admission.

"One is what the Bible allows us," answered Boone.

"I have heard about your Bible," said Gray Eagle. "It is a foolish book."

"Have you ever read it?"

"Warriors do not need to read."

"Then if you've never read it, how can you say it is foolish?" demanded Boone.

"It tells you to have only one wife," said Gray Eagle reasonably.

"It tells us many things," said Boone. "Is that the only one you disagree with?"

"It tells you to worship this man Jesus, who was no warrior," responded Gray Eagle. "His enemies put him to death. What kind of man is that to worship? I would only worship a man who could slay his enemies—a man like"—he searched for an example and finally found one—"you."

"I'm flattered, my brother," said Boone. "But I'm no one to worship."

"You have killed more enemies than Jesus, have you not?" persisted Gray Eagle.

"Jesus didn't kill his enemies," said Boone.

"So he made slaves of them, like this one here once was?" He indicated Pompey.

"No," answered Boone. "He did not make them slaves."

"Then I do not understand."

"That much is obvious," said Boone. "I'm not in the converting business, but one day I'll find a traveling preacher man who can speak Shawnee and have him come by your council house and explain it all to you, everything from the begatting to the miracles." He stretched again. "In the meantime, you still aren't an acceptable substitute for my Rebecca."

"I'm not sleepy," announced Pompey. "I think I'll go visit with Tall Mountain for a while."

"Do whatever you want," said Boone. "I'm not your keeper."

"I don't have a keeper anymore," said Pompey. "Sometimes I wonder why I'm helping you, since your friend

George Washington is what we call a practitioner, and so is Thomas Jefferson, who wrote all those beautiful sentiments in his Declaration but obviously feels they don't apply to anyone who isn't white."

"I'm not responsible for them," said Boone.

"But you're trying to help win the war for them."

Pompey got to his feet and walked over to Tall Mountain, who was standing some fifty yards away, leaning on his spear not unlike the way Pompey's mother told him that the men of her tribe used to lean on theirs.

"Do you see anything out there?" asked Pompey.

Tall Mountain shook his head. "No."

"Then why not come and sleep by the fire?"

"That one cannot see Nightkillers approaching doesn't mean they aren't there."

"But if you can't see them, how will you know they're there in time to do anything about it?" Pompey asked.

"I will know."

"By staring into the dark?"

"By watching what you call the Blue Nimbles," answered Tall Mountain. "Now they are calm. If they become nervous, if they keep testing the wind, if they all turn to face the same direction, I will know."

"You're not going to stay up all night, are you?" asked Pompey.

"You want your mounts in the morning, do you not?"

"Why not just walk them over to the Thunderflame, maybe even tether them to one of his legs. He won't feel it, and surely Nightkillers won't dare approach that close to him."

"The Nightkillers know that the Thunderflame has no fear of them, and indeed has no need to fear them. He will not stop them from approaching, and he has no more interest in the Blue Nimbles than he has in the

Nightkillers. Just as he will not attack the one, he will not defend the other."

"It makes sense," admitted Pompey. "If the Nightkillers annoy him enough, what will he do?"

"Kill them, of course."

"How? Will he use his flame? I'd like to see it, just so if we ever learn to control and move them, we'll know what their capabilities are in battle."

"He may use his flame," answered Tall Mountain. "Or his tail. Or he may simply pick a Nightkiller up in his mouth, reach his neck as high as he can, and then drop the Nightkiller."

"That'd do it," agreed Pompey. "If it didn't kill him, it would at least cripple him." He stared at the huge shadowy shape that was munching contentedly some hundred yards away. "Damn! With all the things they can do, there must be *some* way to march them east and turn them loose!"

But if there was, he hadn't thought of it by the time he finally wandered back to his bedroll and went to sleep.

CHAPTER TWENTY-ONE

The dawn of a new day didn't bring them any closer to solving their problem. The Thunderflame had eaten everything edible in the immediate vicinity, and was now grazing about a quarter mile away. The Blue Nimbles didn't show any sign of restlessness, so they knew there were no Nightkillers in the area.

"It's a puzzle, all right," said Boone, staring at the huge dragon. "I have a feeling I could shoot it in the leg or the belly, and couldn't even penetrate the skin. There are probably ways to get its attention, but if you have to irritate him to do it, do you really *want* something like a Thunderflame irritated with you?"

"I still haven't seen this flame of his," said Pompey. "How far out can he shoot it?"

"I don't know," replied Boone. "Why don't you ask Tall Mountain?"

"I did," said Pompey. Then, in English: "He's not the most responsive man I ever met." Pompey relayed the less-than-useful reply that the size and strength of the flame varied.

"Well, we can't just sit here and hope things will change," said Boone. "Maybe something smaller . . ."

"We're riding something smaller," said Pompey.

"I meant a younger Thunderflame, something that isn't the size of a mountain, something that might be more interested in its surroundings."

"This Thunderflame is interested in its surroundings," noted Pompey. "It eats them."

"You know what I mean."

"Let's hope we can find some dragons who know what you mean, or at least can be taught." Boone dispatched Pompey to ask Tall Mountain where the younger Thunderflames grazed.

"There is a lake about a day's ride to the north and west," answered Tall Mountain. "Usually mothers, especially those with very young ones, stay near the water, so that is where we shall find some of them."

"I wonder why they do that?" mused Pompey.

"Easy," answered Boone. "So the young'un can dive in when Papa goes on a rampage and starts shooting out that flame."

"*Do* the fathers go on rampages?" asked Pompey. "This one seems too placid."

"This one isn't trying to breed a female who's more concerned with caring for the baby she's hatched out than with producing more of them."

"How can you be sure?" persisted Pompey.

"I'm guessing," answered Boone. "But I'm guessing based on a lifetime of observing dragons in the wild. Have you got a better reason?"

"No," admitted Pompey.

"Then we'll assume I'm right until events prove otherwise." Boone turned to Tall Mountain. "Can you lead us to the young ones?"

"Yes."

Boone mounted his dragon. "Then let's get going."

The other three men climbed onto their dragons, and Tall Mountain turned his Blue Nimble to the northwest. "If they're not at the lake, we may come across them sooner."

"I have a question," said Pompey, moving his dragon up until it was walking side-by-side with Tall Mountain's.

"What is it?"

"How old or big do the young Thunderflames have to be before a pack of Nightkillers won't attack one?"

Tall Mountain considered the question for a long moment, then shrugged.

"What kind of answer is that?" demanded Pompey irritably.

"It varies with the size of the Thunderflame, and with the size of the Nightkiller pack," said the Kiowa.

"All right, then," said Pompey. "What's the youngest age at which they are free from attack?"

"Maybe six months, maybe more, maybe less."

Pompey harumphed with frustration.

"What are you trying to find out?" asked Boone.

"I figure once they're immune to attack from a pack of Nightkillers, they're probably too big for us to get them to do anything against their will," answered Pompey. "And from what I can tell, their will seems to consist entirely of filling their bellies."

Boone smiled in amusement. "You're asking the wrong question," he said.

"Fine," said Pompey irritably. "You're the King of the Backwoodsmen. *You* ask the right one."

"I don't have to," said Boone. "I already know the answer. So do you."

That stopped Pompey cold. "I do?"

"Yes, you do," put in Gray Eagle. "But because you have lived in the Long Knives' houses and cities, you do not yet know that you do."

"When I want Delphic oracles, I'll go to Greece," snapped Pompey, and instantly realized that neither Boone nor the Indians had any idea what he was talking about. "All right," he said more calmly. "What is the right question, to which everyone thinks I know the answer?"

Boone turned to Gray Eagle. "Tell him, my brother."

"The question is not how old they must be to withstand an attack, for surely the Redcoats have greater weapons than a pack of Nightkillers." He paused for Pompey to consider that, then continued. "The question that matters is how long they live with their mothers before they go off to live on their own."

Pompey frowned. "Why is *that* the important question?"

"Because until they live on their own, they are dependent upon their mothers—and if they are dependent on anything other than themselves, there is a chance we can make them dependent upon *us*. We are beneath the notice of a fully grown male Thunderflame, but a youngster, still unsure of himself, still protected from the world by his mother, still innocent of what lies beyond his immediate surroundings, it is *he* that offers us the best chance of success."

"But if he's that young, won't he be more vulnerable to British cannonballs and the like?" protested Pompey.

Boone laughed. "I'd wager that even the youngest among these beasts is still heartier than the strongest man we can find." The backwoodsman exchanged smiles with Tall Mountain, then continued. "What we need is something we can work with and learn from. Then we'll worry about the giants."

"It seems to me like you're adding an extra step," said Pompey.

"Fine," said Boone. "You work with the adults. We'll visit you in thirty or forty years and see what kind of progress you're making."

"You know," said Pompey, "there are times when your rustic humor begins to pall."

"The same can be said of your citified, book-read ignorance," retorted Boone. Suddenly he grinned. "But I'm too polite to say so."

Pompey nodded his agreement. "Peace?"

"Peace." Boone pointed toward the east. "The enemy is that way."

In early afternoon they passed through a few small herds of buffalo, and when they were hungry Gray Eagle killed a calf with bow and arrow.

"Why not use your gun?" asked Pompey. "You saw the Thunderflame's reaction—or rather, his total lack of reaction—to it."

Boone pointed to a nearby tree. "See those Darters in the branches?"

Pompey peered at the tree. There were Darters of three or four species, all of which Banshee was studiously ignoring as he rode on Boone's shoulder.

"Yes."

"They're in almost every tree we passed, and every tree we're *going* to pass."

"What's your point?"

"If I fire my gun, they'll panic and fly away."

"So?"

"If they fly away, we lose our best warning sign that Nightkillers are tracking us."

"But there aren't any Nightkillers around here," said Pompey. "Look at all the buffalo."

"We just killed one," said Boone. "Has the herd fled in panic? Prey animals aren't blessed with much brain-power; they tend to flee only when an attack is imminent. If the Nightkillers helped themselves to a big buffalo right now, the rest of the herd would stop running the second the kill was made. They'd know there was enough in one bull buffalo to feed the Nightkillers, and no wild animal kills when it's not hungry. They'd go right back to their grazing, some of them within twenty yards of the Nightkillers, as if nothing had happened."

"Fine," said Pompey. "I defer to your broad experience as a prey animal."

"As a *live* prey animal," Boone corrected him.

They cut off the choicest strips of meat from the calf, cooked them, ate some and packed the rest, and were back riding to the northwest an hour later. Banshee kept flying off to dine on grasshoppers, returning with what Boone considered a smug expression on its face.

By late afternoon they'd concluded that they wouldn't reach the lake by nightfall, so they made camp in a huge open area, where anything approaching them would give them ample warning of its presence. Tall Mountain apologetically explained that he had been up for some forty-four hours and would be unable to stand watch all night. Boone split up the watch between the remaining three.

"Why stand watch at all?" asked Pompey. "We haven't seen a buffalo or an antelope for the past twenty miles."

"If we need protection, it'll be from what's up ahead, not what's behind us," responded Boone.

"I thought there's nothing up ahead but Thunder-flames," said Pompey.

"That's right."

"Well, we both know that Nightkillers don't stalk Thunderflames."

"You've already forgotten what Tall Mountain told us—that they'll prey on infant Thunderflames when they get the chance. Night's the best time to steal one away from its mother."

"Probably you're right," said Pompey. "I just figured the babies would sleep right up against their mothers' legs or bellies."

"Probably they do," said Boone.

"Well, then?"

"You saw how little feeling an adult male has in his legs and belly," said Boone. "I don't imagine the adult females are much different."

"I never thought of that," admitted Pompey. "A quick, silent kill . . ."

"Probably that's not the way it happens," said Boone. "Those nostrils should warn them when anything's approaching. But if the wind's blowing the wrong way, or there are stronger scents in the area, or a baby wanders a few yards away—especially if it wanders *behind* the mother. They don't strike me as being able to turn fast—"

"I get the point," said Pompey. He sighed deeply. "You know, Daniel, I thought I was pretty well educated. Traveling with you has shown me how much I *don't* know, how much I still have to learn."

"You'll learn it a lot faster than I'll learn Chaucer and Shakespeare, or any of those fancy European languages or Indian dialects that you speak," said Boone. "We make a better team this way. I wouldn't learn anything traveling with another Daniel Boone, and you couldn't learn much from another Pompey."

"I wonder if it's possible," said Pompey.

"To learn from each other?"

"No, we've been doing that all along. I meant, I wonder if we'll actually find a way to get the Thunderflames to do our bidding."

"We'd better," said Boone. "I couldn't bring Washington the Indian army he'd hoped for. I can't fail him twice on one mission."

"Your friend Washington asks a lot," said Pompey.

"Considering that we're fighting for our freedom, he has every right to."

"If you feel that way about it," said Pompey, "why didn't you join the army?"

"I'm not good at taking orders, or marching in step," said Boone.

"That was a serious question."

"It was a serious answer."

"Is your friend Washington like that?"

"The exact opposite," said Boone. "When he was a junior officer, he followed his orders to the letter. Now he gives orders to the whole damned army—and don't let some of the defeats you hear about fool you. Any other general would have had to surrender three years ago—even Horatio Gates or Benedict Arnold." Suddenly Boone laughed aloud. "And he does it with the damnedest set of wooden teeth you ever saw."

"Well, if we can't find a way to use the Thunderflames," said Pompey, "maybe we can have him bare his teeth and frighten the British to death."

"I'd feel a lot more confident frightening them with some Thunderflames," said Boone. "Maybe tomorrow we'll figure out how."

Maybe, thought Pompey. *But I sure hope your General Washington has some other options.*

CHAPTER TWENTY-TWO

They were up with the sun, and within an hour they came upon spoor that could only have been left by a small herd of Thunderflames.

"How many do you make it?" Boone asked Gray Eagle.

"Fifteen adults, maybe twenty," answered the Shawnee. "All with young of various ages."

"Yes, I make it eighteen myself. They grazed here yesterday, wiped out that stand of trees, then moved north and west, probably to the lake."

Tall Mountain pointed to more spoor. "Nightkillers," he said. "But they made no kills, made no attempts to kill. That means there are no sick infants in the pack."

"I don't understand," said Pompey. "Wouldn't a sick infant be more likely to stay by its mother, while a healthy one would exhibit a natural curiosity in its surroundings and wander farther away?"

Gray Eagle pointed to crushed grasses about two hundred yards due west, and more to the north. "You see?" he said. "The Thunderflames posted lookouts. The Nightkillers might go after a sickly laggard, but the lookouts would have given warning if the Nightkillers had tried to get past them."

"Makes sense," agreed Pompey. "My mother used to tell me about how African animals did the same thing. Elephants always posted guards at the outskirts of the herd. Come to think of it, so did baboons."

"What are those?" asked Tall Mountain, who had never heard the terms before, and Pompey described them to him.

"Daniel Boone," said the Kiowa when Pompey had finished, "I think your friend is a great liar. Can you imagine an animal picking up things with its nose or drinking through it?" The huge Indian laughed, the first time anyone in the party had heard him do so.

"I've never seen an elephant either," replied Boone.

"But you know they exist."

"You tell me they do, and I can't imagine why you'd lie about it—but I won't know it until I see one with my own eyes," answered Boone.

Pompey was about to answer when suddenly a shadow crossed his path, and Banshee hissed excitedly. He looked up, shading his eyes, and saw a creature flying overhead.

"What the hell is it?" he asked. "It's way too big to be a Longglider, and Skyraiders are even smaller."

"Daniel Boone!" said Tall Mountain excitedly, pointing to the sky.

"I know," said Boone. "I see it."

"My God!" said Pompey. "Is that monster just a *baby*?"

Flying above him in lazy circles was a miniature version of the Thunderflame they had seen the day before—

but "miniature" was an incorrect description, because this dragon was somewhat larger in length and weight than a bull buffalo. Right at the moment it was flying lower and circling directly overhead, trying to get a better look at the strange two-legged creatures that were totally beyond its limited experience. It showed no fear whatsoever, but as it came closer and closer it seemed somehow tenser, and suddenly a thunderous half-hiss, half-shriek split the air. The winged Thunderflame raced instantly to an unseen spot some ten or twelve miles to the northwest.

"Its mother calls," said Tall Mountain.

"Impressive," said Boone when it had flown out of sight.

"It had to weigh a thousand pounds," said Pompey.

"Twelve hundred," offered Gray Eagle.

"Well, now I know where the 'Thunder' in the name comes from," said Pompey. "That was a hell of a warning cry, or whatever it was."

"The babies could be carried thirty or forty miles away on the winds," answered Boone. "The mother's cry has to carry at least that far."

"I think 'impressive' is an understatement," said Pompey. "You only think of them as babies because their parents are so much larger—but one of those babies makes one and a half of our Blue Nimbles. Maybe his skin isn't as tough as his parents but, goddamn it, he can fly! How are you going to control a thousand-pound baby that probably doesn't feel pain and can fly away whenever you annoy it or it gets tired of you?"

"I don't know yet," said Boone. "But if there's a way, we'll find it. Besides," he added, "We don't want to bring the babies back to Washington. We just want to use them to learn on. It's the big ones that'll turn the tide of war. I'd love to see what Cornwallis can do against one of them!"

Probably he'll laugh himself silly when he hears about how we tried to get one to even notice we were alive, thought Pompey. *We might have been better off trying to train Cavedancers. At least we didn't have any trouble getting their attention.*

"Well, let's push on," said Boone. "The sooner we get to the lake, the sooner we can begin studying them in earnest."

The four men urged their mounts on, and in another half hour they came to the Thunderflames. They could smell them for almost fifteen minutes before they were close enough to see them. Creatures that large—especially vegetarians with less efficient digestive systems than carnivores—produced a *lot* of dung.

"Damned good thing they don't worry about enemies," muttered Pompey, making a disgusted face as he rode past one pile after another. "I don't think they could hide their presence if they wanted to."

Most of the trees were totally denuded, and there were large patches of barren ground.

"If they did not seek the water, they would have moved on long ago," remarked Tall Mountain, looking at the surroundings.

"How far afield do they go to eat?" asked Boone.

"As far as they have to," replied the Kiowa. "They seek out the water for the safety of the children, but even the young can go two days, perhaps three, without water if it becomes necessary."

And then they topped a rise and suddenly the entire herd was spread out before them. Pompey counted them quickly, and came up with fifty-three adults, every bit as large as the males—in fact, most of them were noticeably larger—and thirty-seven youngsters of varying sizes. A little more than half still had their wings.

They clustered in a huge grassy plain that backed up to the lake Tall Mountain had described. Dotting the landscape were stands of trees, and every tree had one or two Thunderflames grazing on its branches. The smaller babies were with their mothers, the older ones splashed happily in the shallows of the lake. There were a few other animals—buffalo, deer, something that looks like a cousin to the Landwagons—but they all gave the giants a wide berth. This was Thunderflame territory, and every animal knew it.

"There's our independence right there," said Boone. "If we can figure out how to get them to Washington and turn them loose on the Redcoats, we can end this war in a single afternoon." He noticed Pompey grimacing, and continued: "You don't look convinced."

"Oh, I'm convinced they can win the war in a day if they're properly motivated. I just don't know of anything that'll get them there besides food—and do you know how much food we'd need to carry to get them from here to there? And once they're there, how do we convince them that the Redcoats are the enemy and that we're on the side of right? In fact, how do we anger them enough to attack anyone at all?"

"We use our brains," said Boone. "That's what separates us from the animals."

"In this case, I'd say fifty thousand pounds of muscle separates us from each of them, and it's all on their side."

"Well," said Boone, "we might as well get them used to us. Let's ride among them."

"Let's let them get used to us from a distance first," said Pompey. "These are mothers with young. They might not take as kindly to close proximity as the male did."

"We'll ride down on our Blue Nimbles," replied Boone. "They'll recognize them as fellow grass eaters and won't bother them."

"You hope," muttered Pompey.

"I hope," agreed Boone. "This will also give them a chance to get used to our scent, and the sound of our voices too."

"You're absolutely sure this is what we have to do?" said Pompey.

"If one of the mothers attacks, just have your Blue Nimble turn and run off. Tall Mountain tells me that they can outrun any Thunderflame that ever lived."

"What a comfort," said Pompey grumpily. "Oh, well, let's get it over with."

He urged his mount forward, and was soon trotting toward the herd of massive beasts and their young. Boone and the two Indians let him go for a moment, then had their mounts fall into stride behind him. Banshee decided that this was an opportune time to scout out the female Darters in the area and flew off as they neared the Thunderflames.

Pompey tensed as he rode up to the first gigantic female, but she kept nibbling on the top branches of a tree and paid no attention to him. Soon all four men were riding around the various animals of the herd, speaking in loud voices, seeing if they could elicit any response, even a curious glance.

"We don't seem to be bothering them at all," said Pompey, who was more surprised than he sounded.

"I told you so," said Boone.

"I count nineteen with wings," said Gray Eagle.

"I saw twenty," said Pompey. "You must have missed one."

Gray Eagle trotted his Blue Nimble through the herd, then returned, "We were each right," he said.

"How can that be?" asked Pompey. "There are nineteen or there are twenty."

"There are twenty, but one is in the process of losing his wings," explained the Shawnee. "They will never lift him off the ground again, and in another week, two at the most, they will fall off."

They rode in and out of the herd, giving the dragons a chance to get used to them. Some of the youngsters stared at them with open curiosity, but the adults continued grazing.

"This one must be newly hatched," said Pompey, indicating the smallest of the dragons. "He can't weigh five hundred pounds." He steered his Blue Nimble to get a closer look. "He's kind of cute, actually," he added.

The baby Thunderflame stretched its neck out and stared at him.

"Hi, fella—or girl, as the case may be."

And suddenly the infant flapped its wings and took off, hissing and squealing happily. It reached a height of twenty feet, then flew down right at Pompey, who had no time to duck or to move his Blue Nimble away.

The baby dragon collided with Pompey, knocking him to the ground, then began rubbing its head—small for a Thunderflame, but massive compared to Pompey—on Pompey's chest.

"Get him off me!" yelled Pompey.

"You've made a friend," said Boone, amused. "He's playing with you."

"He's killing me!"

And suddenly Pompey was looking into a far larger face than the baby's. The mother, alerted by the commotion, had swung her neck around, and now her head hovered just above the man and the baby dragon. Her huge mouth opened and Pompey was sure he was about to get incinerated—but the baby kept rolling on the ground next to him and pushing him with its nose and making chirping sounds, and finally the mother decided the two of them were playing and that the baby was under no threat. She slowly straightened out her neck, raised her head, and went back to nibbling the leaves off branches.

"She obviously figured out that you meant her baby no harm," remarked Boone.

"The same can't be said for the harm he's doing me! Give a hand and pull him off!"

"Just ignore him and he'll get tired of it," said Boone. "I'm not strong enough to pull him off. None of us are."

"Damn it, Daniel!" bellowed Pompey. "Get him the hell off me!"

Tall Mountain withdrew a grass rope from his bedroll, dismounted, wrapped it around the neck of the baby—who seemed not to notice it or him—and then got back onto his Blue Nimble. He tied his end of the rope around the Blue Nimble's neck where it joined the withers, then urged his mount to pull the infant Thunderflame off Pompey.

At the first jerk of the rope on the baby's neck, the little dragon let out a squeak of pain and surprise. The mother turned faster than Boone had thought possible, opened her mouth, and shot out a huge blast of fire that encompassed Tall Mountain and his Blue Nimble before they could react. The baby instantly left Pompey and huddled against its mother.

"Jesus!" said Boone, staring at the two charred corpses as the mother and baby walked away, the latter trailing the grass rope behind it. "Jesus!"

Pompey got painfully to his feet. "And we're supposed to train *that*?"

CHAPTER TWENTY-THREE

They dug a shallow grave for Tall Mountain. Boone surprised Pompey by reading solemnly over the grave from a small Bible. When he was done he carefully replaced the Bible in his backpack.

"Seems strange, taking God out in the wilderness with you," remarked Pompey.

"What better place for Him?" replied Boone. "He goes where He's needed."

"Should we do anything about the Blue Nimble?"

Boone looked at the dragon's charred body. "He's more like a Black Not-Very-Nimble now," he said. "We might as well leave him where he fell. I don't think the Nightkillers will bother him; he seems to have been burned clear through."

"That's some weapon these Thunderflames have, isn't it?" said Pompey. "To burn a thousand-pound dragon so thoroughly in two seconds that there's not a piece of un-burnt meat left on the whole body. If we looked closely, we'd probably find that the bones were melted, the way they were on Tall Mountain."

"Even as big as they are, I didn't expect the flame to be that hot or shoot that far," said Boone with grim admiration.

"I'm impressed by how fast she moved," added Pompey. "Nothing that big should be able to turn that fast." He paused and looked at the Shawnee. "What's Gray Eagle doing?"

Boone stared at the Indian, who was sitting on the ground about thirty yards away, assiduously carving a piece of wood with his knife. "He's carving Tall Mountain's tribal totem. When he's done, he'll place it on the grave."

"Like a cross for a Christian?" said Pompey.

"Exactly," agreed Boone. "He believed in his totem. If you had died, we'd have planted a cross over your grave."

"I'd have come back to haunt you," said Pompey. "I practice the religion of my mother's people."

"That's your right," said Boone with a shrug. "I notice you mention your mother all the time, but you never speak of your father."

"I never met him," said Pompey. "At least, I don't think I did. When you're a piece of property, you're never totally sure." He grimaced. "Hell, it could even be a plantation owner or one of his sons or brothers. Most of us have got a white secret or two buried in our pedigrees."

Boone remained silent, whether out of respect or surprise Pompey could not ascertain.

Finally Gray Eagle finished carving, placed the Kiowa totem on Tall Mountain's grave, and joined his two companions.

"Shall we return to my father's territory?" he asked, sitting down cross-legged next to Boone.

"We're not going anywhere," said Boone. "Not yet and not alone."

"But now that you have seen a Thunderflame in action, surely you have no wish to confront another," said the Shawnee reasonably.

"I just got here," said Boone. "I'm not giving up on the first day, or the first week, or the first month. My job is to bring back something that will help tip the scales to the Americans, and now that I've found them, that's precisely what I'm going to do."

"How?" asked Gray Eagle.

Pompey raised his right hand, palm outward. "How," he said.

"This is no time for humor," said Boone severely.

Suddenly they heard a panicky squealing. They looked around but couldn't find the source of it. The sound became louder, more urgent—and finally Boone looked up.

"Well, I'll be damned!" he said. "Look at that!"

A young Thunderflame, perhaps six months old, was flying back toward the herd, perhaps two hundred feet above the ground, but he was being harassed by almost a dozen mature Skyraiders. They couldn't pierce his skin, but they kept swooping toward his head, trying to gouge out his eyes with their claws. The baby lost all sense of direction and began flying north of the herd.

One adult Thunderflame, obviously its mother, began shrieking and hissing at him, and started racing off in the same direction he was flying. She shot her flame at the Skyraiders, but it fell far short, and Pompey saw that the limit of its flame was about fifty feet.

The baby maneuvered awkwardly, trying futilely to elude his attackers, while his mother lumbered on beneath and behind him, her eyes trained on him, paying no attention to the trees and bushes that were in her way.

She simply ran over them, crushing them beneath her massive bulk.

The infant dragon banked steeply to its left and started heading back to the herd. Then the Skyraiders hit upon a new and much more effective tactic. They grabbed each wing in their powerful mouths and hung on. The exhausted youngster didn't have the strength to keep flapping with the extra weight on his wings, and he soon plummeted toward the earth. The Skyraiders hung on until the baby couldn't pull out of his dive, then released their holds and flew off. The young Thunderflame crashed to the ground an instant later.

Its mother reached it in another minute. She tried turning it over with her muzzle, pushed at it with her feet, shrieked into its ear as if to startle it into moving, but it lay still, all signs of life departed.

"What was that all about, do you suppose?" asked Pompey.

Boone shrugged. "Maybe he wandered—or, rather, flew—into their territory and they were defending it. More likely, he inadvertently frightened their young— he's pretty frightening if you weigh ten or fifteen pounds and just hatched out of an egg this week. But it shows why we haven't seen them flying all over. Obviously they have some instinct, which clearly wasn't strong enough in this one, to stay on the ground and not to do any exploring on their own. And when they do fly, they put themselves at the mercy of creatures like Skyraiders who are more at home in the sky. After all, none of the Thunderflames are flying by the time they're a year old."

The baby's mother was inconsolable. She remained with the body for most of the day, whining, crying, hissing mournfully, pushing at it with nose and feet. Finally at night she went off to eat; she did not return to the herd the next morning, and none of the other dragons seemed bothered by her absence.

"Nothing could have killed *her*," remarked Pompey when they noticed she was gone. "I wonder where she went?"

"Something could have killed her," Boone corrected him. "That's why she's got the flame, remember? But my best guess is that she's still alive. With no baby, she's probably in the market for a new husband to fertilize some new eggs."

"You know," said Pompey slowly, "I think I'm getting an idea."

"You're not going home to fertilize anybody," said Boone.

"To hell with you, Daniel," said Pompey irritably. "I'm off to play with my new friend."

And so saying, Pompey mounted his Blue Nimble and rode into the midst of the herd. When he found the infant who had practically killed him with a display of affection, he dismounted and approached it on foot. This time the youngster held some of its enthusiasm in check, merely knocking Pompey down a couple of times by giving him some playful bumps on the chest with his muzzle.

When the dragon had calmed down, Pompey began talking to him in his African mother's tongue. He had no idea why he chose that language; it was just that his mother had always seemed to think it was the best language to use when communicating with animals. He reached out and petted the dragon. Its skin, even at a week or two of age, felt incredibly scaly and rough, and he was sure it couldn't possibly feel his hand, but it wriggled with delight nonetheless.

He spent the next three hours with it. When he saw that his Blue Nimble had wandered away and was grazing about ninety yards away, he began walking toward it, and the little Thunderflame instantly fell into step behind him, butting him playfully with its head. The baby's gigantic mother gave them a quick glance, decided that her offspring was under no threat, and then went back to filling her belly.

When it was time for lunch Pompey rode back to where Boone and Gray Eagle were observing the herd, still followed by the dragon.

"I hope you enjoyed your morning," said Boone.

"Actually, I did," replied Pompey, dismounting. "How was yours?"

"I have been studying them for two days now, and I still haven't figured out how to get them to even acknowledge our existence, let alone obey our orders."

"Maybe you should do what you yourself suggested some time ago, start with the very young," said Pompey. "This fellow here seems more than happy enough to acknowledge my existence."

"So did one of their mothers," said Boone. "We buried the results of that acknowledgment yesterday."

Pompey had no answer for that, or at least none that Boone would accept yet, so he remained silent.

After they ate, Pompey led his companion back to the middle of the herd. Along the way he picked up two more followers, one still in possession of its wings, one— a three-thousand-pounder—without. He befriended them as best he could, and actually had to sneak away at twilight so as not to be followed back to his bedroll and possibly crushed by accident in the dark.

"Everyone's allowed a day off of work now and then," said Boone during dinner. "You've had yours. I could use your help tomorrow. I'm not making any progress at all."

"Of course you aren't," said Pompey. "I've yet to see you approaching one of them."

"It wouldn't make any difference," said Boone. "If I hacked at one of their legs with my hatchet, I'd shatter the blade. If I shot them, they'd pay no attention to the sound or the bullet. If I yelled at them, they'd act as if they didn't hear." He sighed. "I suppose the next step is to walk to the tail, climb up the back and the neck, and see if there's any way to control them from there. Maybe if I spoke directly into their ears . . ."

"What will you say?" asked Pompey sardonically. "Giddyup?"

"At least I'm working on the problem," said Boone, clearly annoyed with Pompey and with his failure to come up with a plan of action.

So am I, thought Pompey, *but if I told you my idea, you'd think me mad.*

CHAPTER TWENTY-FOUR

Luckily for General Washington, just as Boone's hopes had begun to diminish, Pompey had to acknowledge that his own optimism was beginning to increase.

On the morning of their ninth day with the herd of Thunderflames, Boone announced that he was stymied, and that it was time to move on.

"Maybe we can put together a force of two thousand Indians from the various tribes up and down the Mississippi and the Ohio," he said when Pompey and Gray Eagle had joined him around the small fire he'd built. "It probably won't do much good against the Redcoats, but we've got to try."

"That is not our only option," said Pompey.

"If you're suggesting we just stay here and sit out the war—" began Boone angrily.

Pompey shook his head. "I suggest no such thing. In fact, gentlemen, I submit that a solution is right before our eyes, as indeed it has been since our very first day in these parts."

"Explain yourself, man; we have no more leisure for riddles."

"Think back, Daniel," said Pompey. "What happened that first day?"

"How could I forget?" replied Boone. "One of the dragons burned Tall Mountain to death."

"Correct," said Pompey. "And that's the answer, only I didn't realize it at the time."

"We already knew they could shoot flames," said Boone, trying to keep his temper. "What we still don't know is how to make them go where we want and fight who we want."

"Yes you do," said Pompey. "You've just been looking at it the wrong way."

"Enlighten me."

"All right," said Pompey. "*Why* did the Thunderflame kill Tall Mountain?"

"Because she thought he was hurting her baby," said Boone, wondering where this was leading.

"That's right," said Pompey. "If you want to get their attention, all you have to do is make them think you're threatening their babies."

Boone's eyes narrowed as he began to consider the possibilities.

"All right," he said thoughtfully. "We can make the mothers pay attention. But it's the kind of attention that will burn us all to cinders."

"That's why I've been playing with the babies," said Pompey. "I know them all now, and they know me. More to the point, they trust me. Watch."

He put two fingers in his mouth and emitted a shrill whistle. None of the adult dragons paid any attention, but three of the babies, all still sporting wings, began approaching him.

"You see?" said Pompey. "They'll come when I whistle to them. Give me another few days and I can get six or eight of them to come."

"And then the mothers will shriek or hiss, and they'll all go back," said Boone.

Pompey smiled. "What if they can't go back?"

"What are you getting at?"

"What if we build some huge cages, and put them on wagons?" asked Pompey. "I'm sure I can get them to follow me into the cages. I'll walk out between the bars, but they'll be too big. What do you think they'll do?"

"Start sending out some panicky calls to their mothers," answered Boone.

"That's right. The Thunderflames may be huge and powerful, and they may be quick as far as pivoting, but I'm willing to bet they can't run down a Blue Nimble. What if we got Fast Rider and his Kiowas to sell or give us all the Blue Nimbles we saw in his corral, and hitched about half of them to the wagons? We could take the other half along as fresh reserves."

"It's an interesting idea, Pompey," said Boone, "And now I know why you've been spending your time with the youngsters. But they'd catch us. We'd break an axle every few miles, even if the wagons held up, they'd surely catch us at the rivers."

"All right," said Pompey. "There's an alternative—but we can't use all the babies. Only those with wings."

"I don't think I want to hear this," said Boone.

"They're babies, but they're big enough and strong enough to carry a grown man aloft," said Pompey. "What if we make harnesses for them, we teach them to carry us, and we fly off on three of them?"

"Even if you could train them to carry us, they'd get two miles away, the mothers would call them, and back they'd go," responded Boone.

"Not necessarily," said Pompey.

"Explain."

"You've spent most of your life out in the wilderness, so you probably haven't had much to do with horses," said Pompey. "But on the plantation where I grew up, we had almost a dozen horses. And along with the normal bridles, the blacksmiths had invented bridles for horses with tender mouths, horses who didn't want to obey their riders, horses who bore to the left or bore to the right. They came up with something for every problem. For example, if you had a horse who pulled to the left, you fashioned a bridle that would hurt his mouth any time he even looked to the left." Pompey paused. "If they can do that for horses, why can't we do it for Thunderflames?"

"For one thing," said Boone, "you're not talking five-month-old horses whose mothers are whinnying for them."

"And you don't want to get so far ahead of the mothers that they can't find us, or so close that they can catch us," added Gray Eagle, who had been listening intently.

"No one ever said winning a war would be easy," said Pompey. "I've shown you how. Now it's up to you."

"I'll have to think about it."

"No you don't, Daniel," said Pompey. "You know it works in theory, so there's no sense thinking about it any further. Now we have to see if it works in practice."

"Even if it does, will they follow us all the way back East?" mused Boone.

"You saw the mother that first day, when the Skyraiders were attacking her baby," said Pompey. "I think she'd have followed him all the way to England if he'd flown there."

"He's right, Sheltowee," said Gray Eagle. "All that remains is to see if it can be done."

"I know," said Boone, ignoring the use of his Shawnee name. "I know. It's the one way to get the adults moving, and it'll put them in a killing rage. We'll have to plot the course so we don't go near any human settlements, and we have to make sure we land them in among the Redcoats and not our own men." He shook his head. "It's an enormous undertaking. I just don't know . . ."

"It occurs to me," said Pompey, "that after the first hundred miles or so, we'll only need two babies."

"Oh?"

Pompey nodded. "Somebody has to ride ahead on a Blue Nimble and warn everyone of what's coming. The farther east we go, the more likely we are to come into contact with people, and we'll have to warn them off. I think the mothers will be in such a rage that they'll burn or trample anything they see, whether it has to do with their babies or not."

"If we get to that point, that'll be your job," said Boone. "Gray Eagle and I should be better able to control the flying dragons."

"I wish it was my job, but it isn't," said Pompey. "It's yours, Daniel."

"Not me," said Boone. "I'm going to be riding one of the Thunderflames."

"We'll kill it and dispose of the body, so the mother thinks it's still flying with the other two, but you have to be the one to ride ahead."

"Why?" demanded Boone pugnaciously.

"If Gray Eagle or I ride through a town like Paul Revere, warning them that gigantic dragons they've never seen or heard of are coming, what do you suppose will happen?" Pompey asked. "They'll probably shoot Gray Eagle and sell me. There's something else to consider:

Gray Eagle doesn't speak English. That leaves you and me. Who are they more likely to listen to—the great Daniel Boone, or an escaped slave who hasn't even got a Christian name?"

Boone considered the statement for a moment. "You're right, of course," he said Boone. "It'll have to be me."

"Don't look so morose," said Pompey. "Think of all the lives you'll be saving. By the time we reach the towns and villages on the other side of the great rivers, the mothers are going to be in a *very* foul temper."

Boone stared thoughtfully at the herd of dragons. "Will it work, do you think?" he asked.

"I'd be much happier caging them."

"I know. But you'd be much deader too, probably in less than five miles."

"True," admitted Pompey. "I suppose I'll start working on bridles tomorrow, and even if we can't outfit them with saddles, we've got to rig something, maybe just a strap with a couple of loops, that'll act as stirrups, because I figure the first few times we go up they're going to do everything they can to throw us off."

"We'll start by just getting them used to our weight," said Boone. "We'll let them carry us on the ground for a week or two before we ask them to fly—and while I'm thinking of it, how *do* we ask them?"

"We'll train them the way they trained horses back on my plantation. We'll give them a command, and reward them when they get it right."

"How do you reward them if they're flying away?" asked Gray Eagle.

"Watch," said Pompey with a confident grin. He made an odd sound, and suddenly the baby Thunderflames were practically on top of him, pushing him this way and that with their noses. He took some fruit out of his pocket and gave a piece to each. "*That's* how," he said. "I've taught them that they'll be fed a sweet fruit if they come when they hear that sound. We'll train them to do other things too. If I can't find any other way to make them fly, I'll climb a tree and make that same sound, and add another, and eventually they'll figure out that the one sound means food, and the other means fly."

"How long will this take?" asked Gray Eagle.

"I don't know," said Pompey. "As long as it has to. I've only been working with them for a few days."

"You misunderstand," said Gray Eagle. "I do not worry about George Washington, for he is a great warrior. But the babies lose their wings, so I think you should work only with the youngest of them. What is the purpose in training them to carry us aloft if they are wingless?"

"A good point," said Pompey. "I'll work only with the four or five youngest."

"There are only three of us," noted Boone.

"I know, but one of them may prove to be harder to train. Or he could be attacked by Nightkillers. Or the Skyraiders may go after him the way they did with that first baby. It never hurts to be prepared. And there's something else, too."

"Oh?"

"Look at them," said Pompey, waving a hand toward the Thunderflames. "They've got a herd instinct. They're better at following than leading. Who knows? Maybe ten or twelve of the other babies will fly along with us."

"Until their mothers call them back," said Boone.

"Then they'll have to choose between two instincts," replied Pompey. "Who's to say one is stronger than the other?"

Boone was silent for a moment, and then turned to Gray Eagle. "It's not much of a plan, but at least it's something. Have you got any better ideas?"

The Shawnee shook his head. "At least we shall touch the clouds before we die, Sheltowee."

"My name is Daniel, and I'm not interested in dying," said Boone. "All right, Pompey, we'll try it your way. In fact, I think we'll get a little help."

"What do you mean?"

"We're only a day's ride from that Kiowa village," said Boone, "and I hate the idea of weaving grasses into bridles. I think I'll ride back there while you two work with the youngsters. I'm sure I can get the leather for bridles, and I'll wager I can even get Fast Rider and some of the others to join us. I'd rather have twelve or fifteen Thunderflames loose on the Redcoats than just three."

"It's worth a try," agreed Pompey.

Boone walked to his Blue Nimble. "I might as well start now. I should be back by nightfall tomorrow."

"We'll be waiting."

Boone mounted his dragon and began riding off to the southeast, with one thought foremost in his mind, a thought that his friend George Washington shared more and more often:

What a hell of a way to fight a war.

PART FOUR

EPHRAM EAKINS'S BOOK

Chapter Twenty-five

Ephram Eakins led the British on a merry chase. Every time he got more than five miles ahead of them he slowed his men down, and he tried to keep the margin within three miles. He left scouts behind to warn him if the British were making too strong a push, marching at night, putting in sixteen-hour days, doing anything that might close the gap between themselves and Eakins,

He constantly worried that they'd give up and turn back. At one point he had some of his men make an especially clumsy effort to convince the British that they had crossed the river, hoping that when their trackers realized it was a ruse they'd take it as a sign of fear or weakness and continue their pursuit with renewed vigor.

He kept it up for four days. Then his scouts told him that the British had split up, that half of them were back-tracking to the old camp, while the rest were still following Eakins and his men.

He knew that he didn't have enough firepower to successfully ambush even half the British force, so he kept marching. On the afternoon of the sixth day he was informed that most of the remaining Redcoats had turned back, and the force that was tracking him was now less than seven hundred strong.

"Well," announced Eakins to a handful of his men, "we bought General Washington six days, and we still can't go up against the force that's following us, not with only a hundred men. Pass the word that tonight, after it's dark, we'll swim across the river. There won't be a moon, so if we wait about three hours after sunset it should be pitch black, and even if the British are closer than we think, they won't see us."

"They'll see our tracks in the morning and know we crossed, sir," said a sergeant.

"No," said Eakins. "They'll know we *tried* to cross. Remember, they still think the river's full of sea dragons. We won't hide our tracks on this side, but I want to cross opposite a spot where we can climb out without leaving tracks on the other side. Have a couple of men go ahead and see if there's anything like that coming up in the next five to ten miles. A large flat rock would be perfect; if there isn't one, then have them scare up something else that's hard enough so we won't leave tracks, or so overgrown that no one on this side of the river will be able to see that we climbed out. Then rip up any clothes we can spare, soak 'em in the water, and scatter 'em along the shore at the point where we'll be crossing. It worked once; it might work again. At least it'll slow them down while they're deciding if it's a trick or there really are man-eating dragons in the river."

The sergeant saluted and went off to do Eakins's bidding, and the young captain began to give some thought about what to do once he'd crossed the river. He'd move his men inland, of course, so they couldn't be seen from the opposite shore, and then they'd start marching east. Washington was six days ahead of him, but Washington was looking for another army to join up with; he wasn't marching just to get away from the Redcoats. And if he did join up with them, he might not be more than a week's march away. If he came across a major force like Morgan's, he might even reverse course and come looking for the British who had barged across the river.

Then he remembered: Thousands of British were also heading east after Washington. The general had planned to cross the river thirty miles beyond the camp he'd left. That meant there was every chance Eakins would run into the British first, especially if they hadn't wasted a week building more barges.

It was a problem. His orders were to join up with Washington. Washington was to the east. And between them, in all probability, were a few thousand British soldiers.

He was sure there were proper procedures to follow, decisions that every officer knew how to make. But he wasn't an officer, not really; he was just a kid from Pennsylvania that Washington had rewarded with an officer's commission. He wished he was still a corporal, that someone would tell him what to do. He hated the thought of a hundred men depending on him, waiting for his orders. It didn't help that a third of the men had outranked him two weeks ago. They didn't want him to fail, of course; if he made a wrong decision, they were *all* dead—but they were more than a little resentful that they were suddenly taking orders from the Ephrata farmboy.

He started considering his options. He could cross the river as ordered and try to avoid the Redcoats and rejoin General Washington. But if he ran into the British, he was so badly outnumbered that he had only two courses of action: surrender or death.

All right, then. He could march straight north fifty or even a hundred miles, and hope to hook up with some other American force. He'd avoid the British—unless there was another column he knew nothing about, which was a distinct possibility—but it might be weeks, maybe even months, before he found an American unit to join.

He could position his men along the trail on this side of the river and fight the way the Indians did, shooting from cover, fading into the bush, running ahead, shooting again, never showing themselves, fighting a guerrilla battle. But he knew his men didn't have enough ammunition to keep it up, and past experience had taught him that the British were not quitters, that if you shot at them it didn't demoralize them, it just made them more eager to confront you in battle.

The problem was, he didn't like any of his alternatives. He didn't believe in suicidal battles, and he wasn't interested in spending weeks searching for a unit to join.

And then an interesting thought occurred to him: What if he sent ten of his men across the river, and tried to make it look like the whole hundred had gone? It wouldn't be that hard. They could make enough tracks and crush enough vegetation so that it looked like they all swam across. And what if he didn't leave shredded clothes? What if, instead, he did what he could to convince the British that they didn't need a barge, that anyone could swim across the river at this point. After all, it was six days downstream of the camp. Maybe sea dragons didn't come this far downstream. Maybe it was too shallow for them. Maybe they were spawning upstream.

Okay, so he would convince the Redcoats he'd crossed the river, and try to convince them that they could follow suit in perfect safety. Then what?

Then he could take his remaining ninety men, march about five miles south, and then turn east, paralleling the river. His scouts could move ahead and let him know when the main body of British had crossed the river, at which time he could continue marching east in perfect safety. He'd send a pair of his best scouts across the river in forty or fifty miles and see if they could locate Washington. If they could, he'd find a way to join his commander. It might be dangerous, crossing the river when the British were already on the other side and looking for Washington, but it was a lot less dangerous than being on the same side as the British until he could link up with the rest of his army.

The more he thought about it, the better he liked it. He sought out his sergeant, canceled his previous orders, and issued new commands.

When night fell, he had all hundred men walk up to the water over a three-hundred-yard section of the riverbank. The ten who had been selected to swim across began, and the other ninety walked downstream almost a mile in knee-deep water, then marched ashore in single file, the last man doing what he could to obliterate any footprints by dragging a branch behind him on the damp ground.

Eakins couldn't see to the far side of the river, but he knew his men would be marching ashore, walking backward into the water, marching ashore again, and doing what they could to leave the tracks of a hundred men. He wished they could swim back and rejoin him, but in the dark they'd never find the right spot, and he didn't want to leave any clues for the British about what he was up to, so he had ordered them to make their way to Washington's army as best they could.

He marched his men south for almost five miles, then turned to the east. They were well out of sight and earshot of the British, but since he didn't know exactly where the British were, or even that his ruse had worked, he ordered total silence in the ranks. No talking, no singing, and no smoking, for on a night as dark as this, a flame, even a momentary one, could be seen from an enormous distance and could conceivably give their position away.

They marched all night, and in the morning he signaled a halt and passed the word, in whispers, that they had four hours to sleep. Eakins himself remained awake, fine-tuning his plan, looking for weak spots. It occurred to him that the British would be marching by day and sleeping in the dark—after all, they couldn't track the Americans at night—and that he and his men could march by night and sleep by day with less chance of doing anything that might attract the Redcoats' attention.

He'd decided to keep his scouts on a daylight schedule, since all he wanted them to do was let him know where the various British units were. Washington had surely crossed the river days ago, and he had no knowledge of any American troops on this side of it.

Damn! he thought. *I'm doing this by the seat of my pants, and all those men are depending on me to do it right. Even the general's lost some battles and he's the greatest military mind there is. It's downright presumptuous for me to be telling these men what to do.*

And yet, he knew that if someone else was in command and had suggested that they all cross the river as planned, he'd have argued forcefully against it. His gut instinct told him that backtracking on this side of the river was the best way to survive, but he hated the fact that there wasn't a higher authority to issue the order or at least tell him that he was right.

He'd been a lot happier two weeks ago, just working with the Skyraiders. He had an affinity for them, as he did for most animals. He felt a sense of accomplishment when they finally understood what he wanted of them and rushed to obey him, he even liked just sitting around getting to know each of them, their individual temperaments and quirks. If the war was ever over, and if he lived through it—neither of which seemed very likely to him at the moment—he thought that when he went back to the farm in Ephrata he'd like to start raising Skyraiders like Amanda Blakely did. Not to eat—though he had no problem with the prospect of frying up some Skyraider eggs—but just to have them around. Maybe if he did real well he could buy a second farm in Philadelphia, or maybe even on Long Island, and start a messenger service. The newspapers would pay a pretty penny to get news from another state the same day it happened.

The trick, though, was to live long enough to put these fine plans into practice. He knew he should sleep, should try to replenish his energy before they began another all-night march—and if the scouts brought word that the British weren't within ten or twelve miles he didn't plan to wait until dark but would start in midafternoon—but his mind kept racing over all the possibilities and permutations of his plan, all the things that the British might do that he hadn't expected, and how he would react to each.

And then Private Wilson was shaking him by the shoulder, and he realized that he had indeed nodded off.

"It's about an hour before twilight, sir," said Wilson. "The scouts have reported that the British force that was closest to us swam across the river this morning, just like you wanted them to do, and that the main body of Redcoats is well ahead of us, perhaps thirty miles."

Eakins sat motionless for a moment, trying to gather his senses about him. Finally he looked around and saw that almost all the men were awake.

"All right," he said. "Pass the word that they can start fires and cook whatever it is that they want to eat. We leave in an hour."

"Yes, sir."

"Just a minute, Mr. Wilson," said Eakins.

"Yes, sir?"

"I've got some jerky in my pack. Enough for two, if you'd care to share it."

Wilson's homely face lit up. "Thank you, sir. I haven't had any meat since we split off from General Washington last week."

"Maybe if we push a few miles farther south, we can scare up some game," said Eakins.

"I hope so, sir. I've been getting tired mighty easy the last few days. I think it comes from not having much to eat."

"I'm sure it does," said Eakins, opening his pack, pulling out the jerky, tearing it in half, and handing a piece to Private Wilson.

The young man bit into it. "It's mighty hard, sir."

"I know," said Eakins. "I've been carrying it with me for a few days."

"But it's good, sir," he added hastily. "You know, I wouldn't mind this damned war so much if I wasn't so hungry all the time."

"You might cheer yourself up by thinking about what the British are eating—or what they *aren't* eating," said Eakins. "They've outrun their supply lines, they don't know the territory, and they don't dare fire their rifles since they don't know where we are and they don't want to give away their position."

"I hadn't thought of that, sir," admitted Wilson. "I guess it don't make much difference which side you're on. If you're a soldier, you're just naturally going to be hungry from the first day of the war until the day you finally stop a bullet."

"With a little luck we won't be stopping any bullets," said Eakins. "General Washington is always saying he can't win a war with men who died for their country."

"He's a great man, isn't he, sir?" said Wilson. "If we finally win this thing, I can't see anyone but him being king. I come from Massachusetts, but I don't figure Mr. Adams or Mr. Hancock would make half as good a king."

"I think we're fighting this war so we don't have any king," said Eakins. "At least that's what they tell me."

"Who'll rule us then, sir?" asked Wilson.

Eakins shrugged. "I don't know. Whoever it is, all I want is for him to leave me alone and let me work my farm."

"Must be nice to live on a farm, sir."

"Where do you live, Mr. Wilson?"

"My dad's a printer, like Mr. Franklin. We got a house right in the city, and he's set aside most of the ground floor to work in." Wilson wrinkled his nose. "The place always smells awful, especially when he's mixing up a new batch of ink."

"Do you plan to become a printer, too?" asked Eakins.

"I don't know, sir. I been fighting since I was fifteen, and I got a lot of learning to do if I'm to be a printer. I kind of thought I might head West when it's all over, maybe be like Dan'l Boone."

"Do you know him?"

"No, sir, but I heard of him. I guess just about everyone has. They say he's a friend of General Washington."

"That's what I hear."

"If it's so, sir, why ain't he here fighting the British? We could sure use a man like old Dan'l."

"I hear he's out in the territories, trying to round up some help."

"Can't come any too soon to suit me, sir," said Wilson.

"Or to suit General Washington," agreed Eakins. "He can't keep running from the British. One of these days he's going to have to meet Cornwallis and his army on the battlefield."

"Seriously, sir, do you think whatever Dan'l Boone's doing will make a difference?"

"We'd sure as hell better hope it does," answered Eakins.

CHAPTER TWENTY-SIX

Eakins and his troops paralleled the river for the next three days, staying at least five miles south of it. With the British across the river, it was just a matter of making sure there were no stray Redcoats on the south side of the river, and then deciding exactly where to cross it. He tried to figure out where Washington was most likely to be, but it was useless; without Washington's scouts bringing back reports from the north side of the river, there was no way to know if Washington had hard information about where he could link up with other American units, or if he was just wandering aimlessly, living off the land and the charity of local farmers.

It therefore became a matter not of crossing where he hoped Washington was, but rather of crossing where he knew the British weren't. He asked for volunteers, good swimmers, and sent three of them across the river that night. The next morning all three reported that neither the British nor Washington were anywhere within miles.

"We might as well cross the river right now," said Eakins. "No sense waiting until we're being watched."

"Then what, sir?" asked a corporal.

"Well, we know General Washington was marching to the east. We'll head in that direction too. Also, while there's not much population in these parts, as we go east toward Maryland and Virginia, we'll run into folk who are willing to tell us who's passed by and where they were headed." He paused. "I'll miss this forest, though. I'm going to feel mighty exposed when we get back to flat, cultivated land."

"You know, sir," said Lieutenant Fairfax, the only other officer in the group, a mature twenty-year-old sporting the start of a curly beard, "we'd probably make a lot less noise and be much harder to track if we made ourselves some canoes and just traveled on the river."

Eakins considered the proposal for a moment, then shook his head. "Too dangerous," he said.

"More dangerous than all hundred of us marching together through the countryside?" queried Fairfax.

"I think so," answered Eakins. "Everybody knows General Washington. Every man and woman who believes in independence will offer him food and water. But the British aren't going to get any such welcome. Any time they need water, the one place they know to get it is the river. They'll keep close to it for that, and for the fish too. Besides, I don't think we can spare the time, Mr. Fairfax. The Redcoats are looking for General Washington, and if the general has come across any other American units, he's looking for the Redcoats. That means they're going to meet pretty soon one way or the other, and he's going to need all the help he can get."

"Too damned bad there ain't any sea dragons," said Private Wilson. "They could have made life awful easy by gobbling up the Redcoats."

"That depends on whose life you're talking about, ours or the Redcoats'," said Eakins.

"Wouldn't be no sense spilling any tears over *them*, sir," said Wilson. "After all, they're out to kill us."

"They're soldiers, just like us," said Eakins. "They're just following orders. I ain't been educated like some of General Washington's officers have, but I know that if you want to blame someone, you don't blame the soldiers, you start at the source and blame King George."

"Right," chimed in Lieutenant Fairfax. "When we finally win this thing and get rid of the British King George, there'll come a day when *our* King George orders his army to kill someone, and we won't be any more the villains than the Redcoats are now."

"Captain Eakins says we ain't going to have a king," said Wilson.

"Oh, they may call him a prime minister or a president or anything they want, but he'll be a king just the same," said Fairfax with certainty.

"What's the difference?" asked another young man, honestly curious.

"Kings don't run for office," said Fairfax with a smile. "And once they're king, they don't run for reelection and they don't retire."

"That don't sound like General Washington to me, sir," said Wilson.

"So it'll be King Aaron or King Thomas or maybe even King Ben, which I'd personally approve of, but it's going to be King *somebody*."

"Lieutenant Fairfax is wrong," interjected Eakins. "We're not doing all this fighting so that we can replace Fat George with another king."

"Have you been to England, sir?" asked another of the men.

"No, I haven't," answered Eakins. "Hell, I'd never been twenty miles out of Ephrata until the war started."

"If you ain't been there, how do you know he's fat?"

Eakins smiled. "I know General Washington and General Morgan call him Fat George, and so does General Greene, so I assume that's the way he looks—but fat or thin, he's the last king we're ever going to have."

A lone Skyraider flew high overhead, casting its shadow across them.

"Is that one of the ones you got from Mrs. Blakely, sir?" asked Wilson.

"No," said Eakins. "We let all our Skyraiders loose, remember?"

"Could someone else be using it as a messenger service?" continued Wilson.

"Lieutenant Wilcox had a few Skyraiders that would do damned near anything for him," answered Eakins. "But he's with Washington. Who would he be sending messages to?"

"Maybe they sent one out with a scout and it's flying a message back to Lieutenant Wilcox," suggested Wilson.

We couldn't be that lucky, thought Eakins. Just the same, he pulled his whistle out of his pocket and began hitting the same four notes over and over again.

The Skyraider continued flying to the northeast.

"Too bad," said Eakins. "I'd hoped that—"

He stopped in midsentence as the Skyraider banked steeply and flew back alongside the river.

"Play it again, sir!" said Wilson excitedly. "He's listening for it!"

Eakins played the same notes—the summoning call, as opposed to the sending call—and was gratified to see the Skyraider adjust its course and head straight toward him. It landed gracefully about thirty yards away, stared at the men with no show of apprehension, and waited patiently. Eakins finally figured out what it was waiting for, and played the four-note tune on his whistle again. The moment he began, the Skyraider walked directly up to him and raised its leg so he could more conveniently remove the pouch.

"Lieutenant Wilcox has been working with you," said Eakins. "You never knew to lift your foot before."

He leaned over, removed the pouch, reached in and withdrew a single folded piece of paper. "This is from General Washington himself," he announced. "I figure you have the right to hear it in the General's own words, rather than passing it from one man to another." He turned it over to Lieutenant Fairfax, who began reading it aloud.

"'Lieutenant Wilcox, sir—

"'Please inform the general that we have been unable to locate the main body of Morgan's army, but that Thomas Sumter's troops are within three miles of me as I write this, and Sumter wants to link up with our army. In fact, he says he wants to do it immediately, because Cornwallis has joined together about nine thousand men from various divisions and is said to be less than seventy miles away and heading directly toward the general's position. I'll be leading Sumter's men, who number almost two thousand, to our camp, and should be there in less than two days.

"'Major William Dawes.'"

"Well, that's that," said Eakins. "We've got to join up with General Washington. He's going to need every last man of us, if he's to face Lord Cornwallis and twelve thousand Redcoats."

"The message said nine thousand, sir," pointed out one of the men.

"There are at least three thousand Redcoats who have just crossed the river and will be looking to join Cornwallis," Eakins pointed out. "Once the shooting starts, every British soldier within fifty miles will hear the cannons and know where the battlefield is."

"So will every American," noted Wilson.

"True," conceded Eakins. "But they're not professional soldiers, and a fair number of them are opposed to the war and want to remain a colony."

While they had been speaking, the Skyraider had stood stoically in front of Eakins. Now, its patience exhausted, it leaned forward and began probing his pockets with its snout, searching for food.

"Damn, I forgot," muttered Eakins. "Has anyone got anything with them I can give the dragon? Jerky, perhaps, or maybe a fish?"

One of the men reached into his pack and withdrew some jerky. It was quickly passed up to Eakins, who promptly fed it to the Skyraider.

"As long as he's here, we should take advantage of it," announced Eakins. "Has anyone got a pen?"

No response.

"Well, it wouldn't be much use without ink. We'll use a piece of charcoal from the fire to write on the other side of the letter." Wilson picked up a piece and began whittling it to a fine point. "All right," said Eakins. "My writing and spelling ain't none too good. Who've we got that can write a nice neat message and not make too many mistakes?"

"I'll do it," said Fairfax.

"Good," said Eakins. "Say that we want to join up with General Washington, but we don't know where he is. Explain that we're on the river, maybe forty miles east of where the British crossed in their barges nine or ten days ago."

"How's he going to get his location to you?" asked Fairfax.

"He'll send the Skyraider back."

"It may not come this way. Washington could be a hundred miles north of us, and fifty miles east."

"If it doesn't come back, it doesn't come back, and at least we'll have tried," replied Eakins with a shrug. "If it does come back with instructions on how to join the general, it could save us a few days of hunting for him—and those may be days he can't spare if Lord Cornwallis gets wind of where he's at."

Fairfax took the charcoal from Wilson and carefully wrote the message, then folded it neatly and put it in the pouch, which Eakins then affixed to the Skyraider's leg.

"Now what?" asked Fairfax.

"Now we tell it to fly back to General Washington," answered Eakins.

He put the whistle to his mouth and blew a different four-note melody. The Skyraider instantly took off and headed north and east.

"Well, we were right about his general direction," said Eakins as he watched the dragon fly out of sight.

"Let's just hope he don't fly over no Redcoats," said Wilson.

"They don't know he's a messenger," said Eakins. "He looks just like every other Skyraider."

"If they're half as hungry as we are, sir," said Wilson, "they'll shoot him for food—but he'll be dead just the same."

"Not likely," said Fairfax. "Skyraiders fly awfully high."

"So do eagles, but I seen a number of 'em brought down by musket balls, sir," said Wilson.

"There's no sense worrying about things we can't control," said Eakins. "I think we might as well cross the river now. Every piece of information we have says the battle's going to be on the north side of it, and we know that there aren't any British around right at this moment, so it seems like the proper time to go." He turned to one of the scouts. "Is there any place near here that's shallow enough so we can walk across?"

"No, sir," answered the scout. "We're going to have to swim."

"All right. I want three men to make something, I don't care what you call it—a boat, a raft, a canoe—but something to carry our guns and powder across and keep them dry. If they get wet and we find ourselves in a battle in less than a day, they're going to be totally useless. Lieutenant Fairfax, I want you to supervise the making of the boat." He looked at the river. "The current's pretty strong, so it's fair to assume some of you men are going to get pulled as much as a mile downstream. We'll rendezvous directly across from this spot an hour after we begin the crossing. Is there anyone here who thinks he might not be a strong enough swimmer to make it across?" No response. "We don't need courageous corpses. I'll ask again: Is there anyone who isn't a good enough swimmer to make it across, especially with the current the way it is today?"

Two men reluctantly held up their hands.

"Your jobs will be to stay on the shore and spot anyone who's in trouble and signal to the first of us who reach the far bank," said Eakins. "Once we're all across, I want you to go to Amanda Blakely's farm—not the close one, but the farthest one; I'll give you some landmarks to look for—and make sure that she's not been getting messages meant for General Washington and his officers. I *think* we trained the Skyraiders pretty well, but there's always a chance that they'll fly home rather than where they're supposed to go."

"What do we do if there are some dragons there with messages, sir?" asked one of the two men.

"Can either of you read?"

Both men shook their heads.

"Show the messages to Mrs. Blakely and have her read them to you. Then use your judgment. If you think the messages are outdated and no longer important, destroy them. If you think they *might* be important, see what Mrs. Blakely can do about getting one of her Skyraiders to fly them to General Washington. If that doesn't work, have her point you to the nearest patriot who knows how to swim and send him north with the messages."

Both men saluted, and Eakins spent a few minutes giving them general directions for finding the Blakely farms while the first of his men entered the water.

He waited until the raft that would carry the weapons was loaded and the three men and Fairfax began guiding it through the water. The current began pulling it downstream almost immediately, and he realized that they were going to miss the landing point by the farthest margin, since keeping the raft afloat hindered their ability to swim against the current.

Then, when every other man except the two nonswimmers was in the water, Eakins walked in until he was waist-deep and then began swimming. The current was even stronger than he had anticipated. It wasn't like swimming in the creek back home, but he made it across in about ten minutes.

The men all gathered at the appointed spot. They had to wait an extra half hour for Fairfax and his men, who pushed the raft upstream in knee-deep water. Eakins felt like a fool. He'd been so busy giving orders that it had never occurred to him that four men couldn't carry the weapons for ninety-eight men. He realized that he should have sent them first with the raft, and had everyone swim to whatever spot they emerged at. He sighed deeply; there was a lot more to being a leader of men than just outshooting the enemy.

As if to emphasize the point, a quick head count showed him that three men had either drowned or been swept so far downstream that they hadn't been able to make their way back. So now he had to deal with the question: Should he wait for them, or write them off and start searching for Washington's army?

And then there was the bigger question: Did it matter? Could a handful of men, boys really, under the leadership of another boy who'd spent most of his life on a farm, make any kind of a difference against Lord Cornwallis and his twelve thousand career soldiers?

And because he was honest if nothing else, Eakins had to admit that as far as he could tell, the answer was a resounding no.

CHAPTER TWENTY-SEVEN

It began raining, then pouring, and they continued trudging to the northeast, their feet sinking into the mud with each step, their weapons wet, their powder soaked. The rain continued for two days and two nights, and then, just as suddenly as it had started, it stopped.

Eakins knew his men were helpless until they could get their weapons in working order, and he didn't want to march them into any surprises, so he called a halt and sent three scouts out in various directions, hoping at least one of them would make contact, if not with Washington's army, then at least with *some* American army.

He decided he couldn't stay put more than a day—there were always local loyalists, men and women who thought of the army as radical insurrectionists and would have no compunction about telling the British where they could be found. On the morning of the second dry day he once again moved his men in an easterly direction, and then came the news he'd been waiting for:

Washington's army had joined with Sumter's, and they were no more than fifteen miles away.

And indeed, as they drew closer, Eakins could see half a dozen Skyraiders flying purposefully from one location to another, crossing each other's paths like ships passing one another at sea. One flew directly overhead, and Eakins resisted the urge to pull out his whistle and summon it.

When Wilson saw him reach for the whistle and then decide against it, he asked why.

"It's on a mission," answered Eakins. "And since we don't know what its mission is, there's no sense interrupting or distracting it."

"But you summoned one a few days ago."

"That's because we had no idea where the army was, and we were giving them *our* position and asking for theirs. But our scouts have already made contact with General Washington's army. He knows we're here and trying to join him, so there's no need to distract a Skyraider from what is probably a much more important mission."

"Unless it's just a wild Skyraider hunting for something to eat," said Wilson.

"If he is, then he wouldn't know what my whistle meant anyway," said Eakins. "I ain't a betting man, but if I were, given where we are and what we're near, I'd lay plenty of odds that there's a message attached to his leg."

The Skyraider suddenly changed direction and began a long graceful dive.

"You see?" said Eakins. "He heard a whistle and now he's going after it."

"Damn! We must be gettin' awful close, sir!" said Wilson enthusiastically.

Another Skyraider flew overhead, and Eakins watched it fly in increasingly larger circles.

"You know what I think?" said Wilson after watching it for a few minutes. "I think *that's* a wild one. Otherwise he'd have landed by now."

"I wonder . . ." said Eakins.

"Sir?"

"It seems to me that if he was looking for something to eat and he hadn't found anything by now, he'd fly off to search for easier pickings," said Eakins. "I have a feeling he's a messenger"—he pulled out his whistle—"and since no one else has signaled him to land, I think maybe he's been sent with a note for us."

Eakins raised the whistle to his lips and played the simple summoning tune. At first there was no reaction, but as the dragon's circles took him closer, he suddenly swooped down toward Eakins, and a moment later he touched down and walked calmly up to the young man.

"Hey!" said Eakins suddenly. "I know this one!" He pointed to a long scar on the Skyraider's left shoulder. "See that? I named him Pirate because it looked just like the kind of scar he'd get from a cutlass." He walked up and rubbed the dragon's snout. "Hi, there, Pirate. Have they got you working hard?"

The Skyraider hissed gently and stretched its head forward so Eakins could rub its neck. Then the officer knelt down and removed the pouch from the dragon's leg.

"Mr. Wilson," he ordered. "Get this dragon a reward."

"A reward, sir?" repeated Wilson, frowning.

"Something to eat."

"Yes, sir," said Wilson, running off without remembering to salute. He was back a minute later with a strip of meat from the flanks of a deer that had been killed before the rain had begun. Eakins fed it to the dragon, then told Wilson to have the entire unit report to him.

When they had all assembled a few minutes later, Eakins faced them, the message held firmly in his hand.

"This is from General Washington himself," he announced. "I figure you have the right to hear it in his own words, rather than passing it from one man to another." He cleared his throat and began reading:

"'Dear Captain Eakins:

"'My men tell me that you have almost caught up with us. We have made contact with Sumter's army, but Morgan is far from here, in Georgia or the Carolinas, so I am preparing to face Lord Cornwallis with slightly less than four thousand men. Our best information is that we'll be outnumbered by better than three to one, but there is no sense retreating again. The British are simply too close and I suspect that, as of this moment, their men are in better condition than my own and are more capable of a sustained march.

"'We will meet on the field of battle sometime today, or tomorrow morning at the latest. I shall use every bit of skill at my command, every piece of strategy and misdirection that I can devise, but the likelihood is that we simply cannot defeat such an overwhelming force as Lord Cornwallis has massed against us. This is shaping up as the decisive battle of the war. I truly don't think that your presence will change the outcome, so I strongly urge you to stay away. You would only be sacrificing yourselves in what unhappily appears to be a lost cause.

"'Yours very truly,

"'G. Washington.'"

Eakins folded the letter and put it in a pocket.

"That's the message, men," he said. "I have every intention of disobeying General Washington's orders and joining him, but since it is his expressed desire that we stay away, I figure each of you has to make that decision for yourself."

Wilson stepped forward. "I can't speak for nobody else, but I'd sooner die fighting with the general than live as a British subject."

"My sentiments exactly," echoed Lieutenant Fairfax.

"Everyone who plans to go with me to find the general and fight at his side take one step forward," said Eakins.

Every man stepped forward.

"Then it's settled," announced Eakins. "There's no sense staying here. With a little luck, we can hook up with him in two or three hours." He paused. "I'm sure it don't mean much, coming from someone who was just another foot soldier until three weeks ago, but I'm proud of every one of you." He looked over his men. "Have any of the scouts come back yet?"

"No, sir," said Fairfax.

"Damn! I don't want to meet the Redcoats before we join General Washington. Well, we'll just have to do the best we can. I figure our army's in *that* direction"—he pointed to the east—"and that's where we'll be heading. I want two volunteers to go out ahead of us, and if you see the Redcoats, give us some kind of warning before we march right into them."

"What kind of warning, sir?" asked one of the men.

"If you've got anything better than a gunshot, I'd be happy to consider it."

Seven men raised their hands.

"You and you," said Eakins, indicating two of them. "Head off right now. We'll be on the move in another twenty minutes."

The men took off at a trot.

"Everyone check your weapons," said Fairfax. "Make sure they're loaded, and make sure you've got enough powder if we go into action before we join the general."

They milled about for a quarter of an hour, and then Eakins announced that it was time to go.

"If you get separated," he said, "remember: Watch the Skyraiders. The Redcoats aren't using them, and they haven't figured out that we are or there'd be gunshots every time one appeared in the sky, so just figure out where they're landing, and you should have no trouble finding the Americans."

They began marching. After two hours they hadn't seen any sign of either side. Then one of the two volunteers returned to tell them that the American army was a mere two miles ahead of them. The men were so elated that they practically ran the remaining distance, and in another quarter hour they finally, after many days and many hardships, rejoined the main body of Washington's army.

Eakins requested an audience with Washington, which was immediately granted.

"Captain Eakins!" said Washington. "I'm very glad to see that you and your men survived, but I'm somewhat distressed to see you here. When the Skyraider returned without the message I had sent, I assumed it had reached you."

"It did, sir."

Washington frowned. "Then why are you here?"

"You're outnumbered, sir," said Eakins. "You need every man you can get."

"I need more than that," said Washington grimly. "I need a miracle." He pointed to a high ridge two miles to the north. "Behind that ridge Lord Cornwallis is preparing somewhere between ten and twelve thousand British soldiers to mount an attack. He's spread his men in a large semicircle so that most of our paths of retreat are cut off."

"What about going back the way we came, sir?" asked Eakins.

Washington shook his head. "Our best information is that Banastre Tarleton and a company of fifteen hundred British regulars has been tracking you for the past week. They're probably no more than thirty miles behind you even as we speak." He took a deep breath, let it out slowly, and looked across the landscape. "My guess is that the major attack will come from the right, where the land provides them some cover. But wherever it comes from, we're going to have to stand our ground. There's simply no place to go."

"Then we'll be proud to stand it with you, sir," said Eakins.

"Our only real hope—and it's not much of one—is to contact Nathanael Greene. He's leading a force of almost two thousand, and my understanding is that he's trying to join up with us, but I have no idea where he is. All I know is that he's somewhere to the west, but it could be just beyond the first hill, or it could be five hundred miles."

"We can send the Skyraiders up to look for him, sir," suggested Eakins.

"What good would it do?" asked Washington. "Nate Greene doesn't know we're using Skyraiders. We can attach all the messages we want, but he'll never whistle them down."

"Sir, if he's as hungry as we are, there's a chance his men will shoot one of them down for food, and once they do that they'll find the message."

"Why would the Skyraiders fly to the west instead of some other direction?"

"They wouldn't," said Eakins. "Not necessarily. But if we turn all of 'em loose, we can figure at least three or four will head off in General Greene's direction."

"Well, I suppose it's worth a try," said Washington unenthusiastically. "You're the one who trained them,

Captain Eakins, so I'm putting you in charge of the operation. I'll have as many messages as you need delivered to you as quickly as possible."

"Yes, sir," said Eakins, saluting and then walking to the area on the outskirts of the camp where the Skyraiders were kept in their cages.

Lieutenant Wilcox was there with them, and he greeted Eakins warmly.

"Glad to see you made it back," he said. "From what I hear, we can use all the help we can get."

"That's what they tell me," replied Eakins. "How many Skyraiders are available for duty right now?"

"Three are out, so that leaves twenty-one. How many does the general need?"

"All of 'em."

"All?" repeated Wilcox, surprised.

"From what I hear, if they don't deliver their messages today, there might not be anyone left to receive the replies tomorrow."

Wilcox nodded. "The general's got a point. Will you settle for twenty?"

"If I have to. Why?"

"I've grown real fond of the one we named for John Alden. If things go badly, I'd like to set him free at the last minute and give him a chance to get away."

"He won't, you know," said Eakins.

"With no one to whistle for him, I was hoping he might fly all the way back to Amanda Blakely's," said Wilcox.

Eakins shook his head. "With as many dead men as there'll be on the battlefield, he'll stay here feeding on them and on the rats for weeks. By then the Redcoats will know what we were using the Skyraiders for, and will probably shoot him so they can see if he had any message attached, something that might give them a clue where to find General Greene's army, or maybe Light Horse Harry Lee."

Wilcox sighed unhappily. "You're probably right, but I'd like to hold him back anyway. I've spent more time working with him than any of them others. If we somehow live through this, you won't believe some of the tricks I've taught him to do."

"Hold him back," said Eakins. "If twenty isn't enough, then probably twenty-one isn't either."

"Thank you, Ephram."

A runner arrived just then, carrying the notes Washington wanted attached to the dragons.

"You'd better do it quick," said the runner. "A couple of our scouts just came back and report that the Redcoats are starting to move."

Eakins and Wilcox began putting the messages in the carrying pouches. When they were done they led the Skyraiders out to an open area, pulled out their whistles, and played the simple four-note tunes that sent them on their way.

Twenty winged dragons took off at once, and were soon flying high overhead.

"They make a beautiful sight, don't they?" said Wilcox. "I've really enjoyed working with them. They've become like pets to me. I hope they can stay clear of the fighting."

"I just hope a few of them can find General Greene's army," said Eakins.

"Or General Gates, or General Arnold, or Light Horse Harry, or—" Suddenly Wilcox stopped speaking, shaded his eyes from the sun, and peered into the sky. "What the hell is *that*?"

"What the hell is what?" asked Eakins.

"I don't know, but I've never seen anything like it."

"I see it now!" said Eakins. "It's too burly to be a Skyraider, but the wings aren't long enough for a Longglider."

"There's something else strange about it, too," said Wilcox. "Something on its neck or shoulders."

"A lump of some kind," said Eakins. "It's wobbly, though, like it doesn't belong there."

Suddenly the creature veered crazily to avoid one of the Skyraiders, and the lump fell off and began plummeting toward the ground.

"My God, it's a man!" exclaimed Eakins.

The man hit the ground a quarter mile away with a bone-crunching thud that the two men could hear from where they were. They raced across the intervening distance and soon reached his side.

"It's an Indian," said Wilcox. "I've never seen one from this tribe before."

"Neither have I," said Eakins, kneeling down next to him.

"Is he dead?"

"He will be in another minute."

The Indian's lips moved, and Eakins leaned over so his ear was right next to the dying man's lips.

"What did he say?" asked Wilcox as the Indian jerked spasmodically and then lay still.

"I didn't understand his language," said Eakins, getting to his feet. "But I understood two words."

"What were they?"

Eakins frowned in puzzlement. "Daniel Boone," he said.

CHAPTER TWENTY-EIGHT

How did *he* know who Daniel Boone is?" said Wilcox.

"I've got a better question for you," said Eakins. "What the hell was he riding on?"

"I don't know," said Wilcox, looking up at the sky. "But here comes another one!" Eakins looked up and saw another strange winged beast, flying in haphazard patterns and doing its level best to dislodge its rider. A small Darter flew just above the rider, hovering as if trying to land on his shoulder and being unable to.

"Whatever it is, if it was a horse it'd be trying to buck him off."

"You ever see an animal like that, Ephram?" asked Wilcox.

"Never," replied Eakins.

"He's going to throw his rider."

The creature banked sharply to the left, then arched up and, just as suddenly, went into a steep dive.

"It's coming this way!" said Wilcox.

"It's got to pull out of it fast or it's going to kill them both."

"Maybe the rider can leap off when he's low enough."

"At that speed?" said Eakins. "That'd kill him as surely as if the creature hits the ground headfirst." He peered intently. "This one ain't an Indian. He's dressed all in buckskins."

"Yeah, I can see now. You suppose he's a white man?"

"We'll find out soon enough," said Eakins, as the creature spread its wings out and began drifting down the final hundred feet toward the ground. "Have your gun ready."

"But if he's a white man . . ." began Wilcox.

"Being white don't make him American," said Eakins. "And we know Cornwallis is heading this way."

The creature touched down and the rider hopped off, holding the end of a grass-rope bridle. The animal hissed and bleated endlessly, emptied its bowels and bladder, and trembled incessantly, as the Darter finally landed on the man's shoulder.

"Damned thing's scared to death," said Eakins as he and Wilcox approached the rider and his mount.

"Hold it right there, mister!" said Wilcox, leveling his rifle at the man.

"Put that away, son," said the man. "Where's George Washington? I've got no time to lose."

"That's not a piece of information we're inclined to give out to strangers," said Eakins. "Who are you?"

"My name's Daniel Boone," he said, his voice filled with urgency. "Now take me to Washington!"

"You know, he looks kind of like the drawings I've seen of Boone," said Wilcox.

"What are you doing here, and what is that thing you're riding?" demanded Eakins.

"I haven't got time to explain!" said Boone. "If you don't want every last American soldier to die in the next half hour, you've got to take me to Washington!"

"I didn't think the British were that close yet," said Eakins.

"It's not the British that'll be doing the killing!" said Boone. "I've got to find Washington and have him turn his sharpshooters loose on these damned Skyraiders!"

"What are you talking about?" said Eakins. "Those are *our* Skyraiders."

"What do you mean, yours?"

"We've trained them," answered Eakins. "We use them to carry messages."

"Well, I'll be damned!" said Boone. Then: "You've got to call them off right now! Make them land!"

"I can call some of them. The rest are too high up or too far away."

"We've got to get them all out of the sky or Washington and his army are doomed!"

"I don't understand," said Eakins. "What are you talking about?" He pointed to the baby Thunderflame. "This thing isn't going to kill anything. He's no bigger than a Landwagon, and he's scared to death."

"He's a *baby*!" said Boone. "His mother is bigger than anything you can imagine! We've flown more than twenty baby Thunderflames here just ahead of their mothers, who are in a killing mood. You don't have anything that can stop them. Neither do the British. The plan was to fly them to the British lines and land just behind them. The mothers will go through anything that stands between them and the babies."

"Then what's the problem?"

"Your Skyraiders," said Boone. "The babies are terrified of them. We can't control them, and a lot of them are flying in this direction. Their mothers can't be more than a couple of miles behind."

"But the Skyraiders aren't going to attack something as big as what you're riding," protested Eakins, wondering why Boone seemed so certain that there was a problem.

"*These* aren't," answered Boone. "But they do it back where we found the herd, and the babies don't know they're safe. They panic the second they see a Skyraider. We're running out of time, son! Call them back!"

Eakins took his whistle out of his pocket and played the summoning tune five times in succession. Within half a minute sixteen Skyraiders were racing back to him, floating gently down to the ground.

"Lieutenant Wilcox, reward them and put them in their cages," ordered Eakins.

"Take my Darter, too, just in case one of the Skyraiders takes it in his head to attack," said Boone, handing Banshee to Wilcox. "Put him in a cage until I get back."

Boone began struggling with his mount, which went into a blind panic as the Skyraiders began returning. It took all of his skill to keep it from damaging itself or flying off, but somehow he managed.

"There are four that are too far away to hear," announced Eakins.

"What direction did you send them?" asked Boone.

"I don't know."

"*What?*" bellowed Boone. "How can you not know who you sent messages to and where they are?"

"It was an act of desperation," said Eakins. "Lord Cornwallis is about to attack with an overwhelming force. We sent the Skyraiders out with a general message in the hope some American force would shoot one down. Even if it was too late to help us, they'd at least know what happened to us, and where Cornwallis was on this particular day."

"We've got to get them back!" said Boone. "You're between the Thunderflames and the Redcoats. We had planned to make a sweeping circle around you if you were in the way, but now the babies are going to panic and start dropping out of the air before they reach the British." He reached out a hand. "Give me that whistle and show me how to call them back. Maybe I can reach them before the rest of the Thunderflames spot them."

"Can you guide a panicky dragon with one hand?" asked Eakins. "You can't just stick the whistle in your mouth. It's more like a flute. You'll have to hold your fingers over the right holes. And you'll have to remember the tune. They've been trained not to respond to any other tunes, in case the Redcoats catch on to what we're doing and try to call them off."

"I'll have to manage," said Boone.

"Not necessarily."

"Explain yourself."

"You need two hands to guide a terrified dragon," said Eakins. "I only need one hand to hold on to you while I'm playing the tune with the other." He looked at the baby Thunderflame, which was calming down a bit as Wilcox finished leading the Skyraiders to their cages. "Can he carry double?"

Boone spent a few seconds considering the young man's proposal, and then nodded his assent. "Let's find out," he said. "Hold his head."

Eakins reached up and grabbed the bridle, steadying the infant dragon while Boone clambered onto the Thunderflame and began adjusting his position so that his feet didn't interfere with the creature's wings.

"All right," said Boone, taking a firm grip on the reins. "Get on behind me."

Eakins used the left wing as a ramp, walked right up it, and positioned himself behind Boone. He reached out with his left hand and took a firm grip on Boone's belt.

"I'm ready," he said.

"Then let's go," said Boone. He did something Eakins couldn't follow with his hands and feet, some kind of signal or command to his mount, and the Thunderflame took off, circling higher and higher, shooting panicky glances in every direction as it looked for Skyraiders.

"How big are the grown ones?" shouted Eakins, trying to be heard above the wind and the flapping of wings.

"You'll see soon enough."

"Why didn't you fly *them* here? If they're half what you say, they couldn't be scared of Skyraiders."

"The wings fall off before they're a year old," said Boone. "Believe me, nothing could lift a grown one off the ground."

The Thunderflame started twisting and hissing, and Eakins saw two Skyraiders about half a mile to his left. He immediately put the whistle to his lips and played the summoning tune. The Skyraiders appeared confused for a moment, because they'd never heard the whistle coming from a height before, but then they both altered course and glided down to where Wilcox was waiting for them.

"Two to go," said Eakins.

"One," Boone corrected him. He tried to point straight ahead, but the Thunderflame banked and dove, and he needed both hands to hang on. Eakins tried twice to put the whistle to his mouth, but both times he found he needed to hold on to Boone with both hands. Finally the Thunderflame leveled out enough for him to play the re-call tune, and the Skyraider headed back toward Wilcox.

"There's only one left, unless we run into some wild ones, and I haven't seen any in these parts," said Eakins. "Will one lone Skyraider make them impossible to control?"

"I don't know, but once you see the parents, you'll know why we can't take the chance. Broken Nose and I were a few minutes ahead of the others, but they'll be here any time now, and believe me, son, you don't want them swerving toward your lines the way the first two did."

"Broken Nose?" repeated Eakins as he scanned the sky for the last Skyraider. "That was the Indian?"

"Right."

"I never saw one with his markings and totem before," said Eakins.

"He was a Kiowa."

"A Kiowa?" repeated Eakins, surprised. "You've been leading the mothers *that* far?"

"Yes. We've flattened more than a dozen towns, but we managed to warn the people before it happened."

"So all the riders are Kiowas?"

"No," said Boone. "We've got an American, an escaped slave, a Shawnee, and the Kiowa—a real international force. We *all* want the British out of here." He was silent for a moment. "Look off to your left, son. Here they come."

Eakins looked and saw almost two dozen baby Thunderflames. He couldn't make out the identity of the riders, but they were flying in almost a military formation. Then four of them broke off and headed back the way they came in a large, sweeping arc.

"Something's spooked 'em," said Eakins. "But I can't see the Skyraider."

"No, they're just circling back to make sure the adults are on the right track. They'll make certain they've been spotted and then rejoin the others."

"Maybe the Skyraider's already so far away that they'll never see him," said Eakins.

"Is that likely?"

Eakins considered the question. "No," he said at last. "No, it isn't. He doesn't have any location to go to, so he'll make larger and larger circles until someone summons him or shoots him."

"Damn!" said Boone. "We haven't seen him since we went aloft. That means he's probably due back just about the time the babies are over your troops."

Eakins looked back at the Thunderflames. They were headed north, and would be over the British army in another two minutes.

Just stay away a little longer, thought Eakins. *Just three or four more minutes. Then you can come back and it won't make any difference.*

He thought they'd made it. For ninety seconds the baby Thunderflames continued their northerly flight— and then the lead dragon squealed in terror and peeled off, heading straight for Washington's lines. Two more followed him, and finally Eakins could see the last Skyraider come into sight, circling in from the north.

"Quick!" yelled Boone. "Play your song!"

"I'll try," said Eakins. "But I don't know if he can hear it above all the racket the babies are making!"

He lifted the whistle to his lips—and suddenly the Thunderflame he was riding banked hard to the right. Eakins began slipping off, and felt his grip on Boone's belt coming loose. He waited until he knew he'd lose hold in another second, and then he dropped the whistle and grabbed on to Boone with both hands.

Boone straightened the Thunderflame out, and as Eakins regained his position he got one quick glimpse of his whistle falling toward the earth.

CHAPTER TWENTY-NINE

Well?" said Boone. "I don't hear anything."

"You're not going to," said Eakins. "I lost the whistle."

"Can you sing it or hum it?"

"No," answered Eakins. "He's been taught to only respond to the whistle."

"Did you see where it fell?" asked Boone.

"It'd be like looking for a needle in a haystack."

"All right, then," said Boone. "Reach around and pull out the hatchet I'd got tucked in my belt."

"You can't throw a hatchet and still control the Thunderflame!" said Eakins. "He's been fighting you since the Skyraider came into view!"

"*I'm* not going to throw it," answered Boone. "*You* are."

"Me?" exclaimed Eakins. "I've never thrown a hatchet in my life!"

"You'd better be a quick learner, because I haven't got a second one," said Boone. "You're going to have one

247

chance to knock him out of the sky, and if you miss, God
help Washington and his army."

Eakins snaked his hand around Boone's waist and
came into contact with the hatchet. He pulled it out and
tried to get used to the feel of it, its weight and balance.
It felt strange in his hand, awkward and alien.

"You've worked with Skyraiders," said Boone. "You
know them better than I do. I'll maneuver the Thunderflame as best I can, but I need to know what you'll be
aiming for."

"Give me a second to think," said Eakins.

*Where do I throw it? His head? That would kill him—if I
didn't miss, and if it didn't hit bone and bounce off, and if it hit
blade first. That's an awful small target. His belly? It could do
some damage, but it wouldn't be fatal and might not even make
him land. The legs? No, he doesn't use them in the air; wound
a leg and he'll have even less reason to land. What's left? It's
got to be the wing.*

*Where on the wing? Close to the body? No, he's got too
much bone and muscle there. The tip? I'd most likely miss.
Probably I should aim for the middle; it's not as strong as near
the body and not as hard to hit as the flapping tip, and if I'm
off by a foot or two I'll still hit something.*

*Top, bottom, or head-on? It can't be head-on, because Boone
will never get the Thunderflame to go directly toward him. Is
one side of the wing more vulnerable than the other? Damn it
to hell, I just don't know!*

*Wait a minute! The answer's right in front of me! If I throw
it from beneath him, most of the force will be used up just getting it there. If we're above him and I throw it down, it'll pick
up speed and hit him even harder!*

"Can you take the Thunderflame up above the
Skyraider?" he asked aloud.

"I don't know," answered Boone. "He's pretty scared.
All he wants to do is get out of the sky." He maneuvered

the Thunderflame's head so that it was pointing up. "What the hell—let's give it a try!"

He turned the baby dragon away from the Skyraider. Once it was out of the Thunderflame's field of vision, it became more responsive to Boone's commands, and soon it began climbing until it had reached an altitude of almost six hundred feet. Then Boone had it bank to the right, in a large, lazy semicircle.

"Get ready!" said Boone. "He's going to see the Skyraider and start balking in just a second!"

"The Skyraider's still two hundred feet below us!" shouted Eakins. "We've got to get closer!"

"I'll do what I can, but be ready to throw it when I tell you I can't control him any longer!"

The Skyraider ignored the Thunderflame. It wasn't prey and it wasn't predator; it was just something else in the sky, something that was too high to cause any traffic problems.

"Quick!" said Boone. "Which hand do you throw with?"

"My right."

Boone had the Thunderflame circle and bank to the right so Eakins wouldn't be throwing across his body.

"He's going to bolt any second!" shouted Boone. "Throw it now!"

"We're too far away!"

"It's our only chance! Throw the damned thing!"

Eakins got the Skyraider in his sight. He tried to adjust for the speed it was going, the speed he himself was going, the wind, everything—but then he felt the Thunderflame's body tense, and he knew he had just a second before it rolled and raced away. He wished he had time for a short prayer, but he knew he didn't. He leaned far over and hurled the hatchet.

The Thunderflame jerked against Boone's restraint and began climbing, and suddenly Eakins was so busy hanging on that he couldn't see if the hatchet had hit its mark.

"Straighten out, damn you!" muttered Boone, trying to manipulate the bridle.

"Get him level quick!" yelled Eakins. "I'm starting to slide off!"

"Which side?"

"The left!"

Boone leaned to his right and got the Thunderflame to bank to the right. This gave Eakins a chance to shift his weight and get back behind Boone.

"Did I hit him?" he asked when they had straightened out.

"I don't know. I've been too busy trying to control the Thunderflame." He looked down. "I don't see him."

"Wait a minute!" said Eakins. "There he is, landing by those trees!"

"I think you're right!" said Boone. He looked at the other Thunderflames, which were coming under their riders' control. "We did it—and not a second too soon!"

"What now?" asked Eakins.

"Pompey and Gray Eagle will lead the rest behind the British lines. Then they'll just hover there where the adults can see them."

"Are you going to join them?"

"Of course."

"Set me down first," said Eakins.

"The Thunderflame can carry both of us," said Boone.

"I know—but that Skyraider wasn't hurting or threatening anyone. It's not his fault that the baby Thunderflames are scared of him, or that we had to knock him out of the sky. I want to see how badly he's hurt and do what I can to save him."

"You're a good man, Mr. Eakins," said Boone. "I'll set you down as close to him as the Thunderflame will land."

"Thank you, sir," said Eakins.

"It's Daniel," replied Boone. "Only officers are sir." Then he added: "Sir."

The Thunderflame landed about a quarter mile from the wounded Skyraider. Eakins jumped off.

"I'll see you later," said Boone, as he prepared to go aloft again. "We've got a war to win."

"Good luck, Daniel!"

"We're not the ones who will need it," said Boone as the first frantic hisses of the adults came to their ears.

CHAPTER THIRTY

The first Thunderflame opened her massive mouth and shot out a sheet of fire that incinerated the closest Redcoats. The British fired their rifles at point-blank range, but to no effect. First one, and then four, and then eight Thunderflames raced through their front ranks, crushing dozens of brave men, setting fire to hundreds more.

Cornwallis realized almost instantly that normal firearms were useless against the monstrous creatures. He ordered all his cannons trained on the lead Thunderflame. The first cannonball bounced off, but the second knocked her off her stride, and two more put her down on her side.

The British regrouped behind their cannons and began firing into the Thunderflames. Two more went down, and the remainder hesitated, looking disoriented. Nothing had ever done them any harm before, and suddenly three of their number had been mowed down by the machines that made the awesome clapping noises.

"This can't be happening!" said Boone from his position high above the battlefield. "I didn't lead them all this way just to have the British turn them into targets. If they'd just keep charging, they'd mow right through them. They could melt the damned cannons if they'd try."

Another Thunderflame fell over on her side, thrashing weakly.

"We're going to lose!" muttered Boone. "I can't believe it!"

The Thunderflames had completely stopped advancing, and were looking around in confusion. They were clearly on the verge of panic, and finally the last one in line turned and began racing back the way she had come, hissing and squealing piteously.

"Another five minutes and it'll be over," said Boone. "He's got to think of something!"

"Who?" asked Eakins.

"Washington!" said Boone. "I'm just a backwoodsman. He's the general. It's up to him."

And Washington hadn't been idle. He surveyed the carnage and realized that the battle was going against him. He knew he didn't have the firepower to go up against the British, and he was sure the Thunderflames couldn't tell friend from foe.

He studied the battlefield, forcing himself to remain calm until he could finally spot a way to turn the tide— and then he found it.

"Look!" said Boone, pointing to a lone man racing over from the American lines. "He's figured it out!"

"That's Wilcox!" shouted Eakins.

"And he's got a Skyraider with him!"

For indeed, Wilcox was leading his pet Skyraider, John Alden, by a long rope around the creature's neck. He wasn't charging the British, who were preoccupied with the gargantuan Thunderflames facing them, but instead circling around behind them, where Pompey, Gray Eagle, and the Kiowa had landed their mounts. The babies had grown calm once they were out of the sky and away from the Skyraiders, but now, when they saw John Alden, then began squeaking and squealing in terror—and the adults went wild.

Instinct took over. They charged as one, flames shooting out and destroying the cannons, cooking flesh and melting bone, trampling courageous men beneath their massive feet.

The carnage was unimaginable. Two thousand Redcoats died in the first minute. Three thousand more died in the next minute. Cornwallis knew his cause was lost and was ready to surrender, but he didn't know how to surrender to a group of enraged twenty-ton beasts. Finally Boone spotted him, guided his Thunderflame to the ground, and approached the British commander.

"Sir," he said, "I represent General Washington. Do you surrender?"

"I do, sir," said Cornwallis.

"Unconditionally?"

"Unconditionally."

Boone signaled to Pompey and Gray Eagle, and a moment later they had led the Kiowa and their dragons back over the British lines, landed in front of the adults, and quickly dismounted.

As Boone had suspected, all fury dissipated the moment the reunion commenced. The Kiowa were in no danger thereafter, and neither were the British. Indeed, within a few minutes the Thunderflames paid no more notice to the humans here than they had in their home territory.

Boone escorted Cornwallis to the American lines, where he signed the formal documents of surrender, and the United States of America became the first nation in history to militarily dissolve all ties with the colonial power that had previously ruled it.

"Magnificent beasts!" said Washington when Boone escorted him to where the Thunderflames were grazing. "Just magnificent!"

"They shortened the war, that's for sure," said Boone.

"Shortened it?" repeated Washington. "They *won* it! There's no question about it, Daniel. I shall have to find the proper way to commemorate their efforts."

"While you're rewarding efforts," said Boone, "there's a young officer who is actually responsible for the success of today's battle—a Captain Eakins."

Washington looked inordinately pleased with himself. "Ephram Eakins!" he said. "I saw something in that boy from the start. Would you believe he was a private just two months ago?"

"Well, whatever he was then, he's a hero today," said Boone. "Buy me a drink and I'll tell you all about it."

"Daniel, my old friend, you're on," said Washington, leading Boone back to his tent, where he pulled out a bottle he'd been saving for this day, and which, three hours ago, he was sure would never be opened.

EPILOGUE

Not all the British got word of Cornwallis's surrender, and the war actually dragged on another few months. It was mostly a mopping-up exercise, and Washington showed great patience in negotiating honorable surrenders for his enemy's armies. Morgan actually fought a pitched battle in North Carolina, but for the most part the end of the War of Independence was bloodless.

The Thunderflame adults and infants remained where they were, as no one knew a way to get them to return to the West. Eventually they wandered down to the Ozark range in search of food, where their descendants remain to this day.

George Washington was named the first president of the United States by acclamation. He was offered the title of king, turned it down, and served two four-year terms, retiring to Mount Vernon to live out the final years of his life. He died in 1799.

Daniel Boone moved his family west, first to Kentucky, and then to Missouri when President James Monroe made him a gift of one thousand acres in Fort Osage in 1815, near the present-day location of Kansas City. Never content to stay in one place, Boone, though a very old man, led treks to Nebraska and Oklahoma, and died in 1820.

Pompey never returned to the new nation he had helped to found, but remained with the Shawnee. He married an Indian woman, sired two sons and three daughters, and died of unknown causes in 1814.

As for Ephram Eakins, he formed a partnership with James Wilcox, and went into the business of raising dragons for commercial use, which encompassed every-thing from supplying food to scores of restaurants to creating a messenger service used by the newspapers in Boston, New York, Philadelphia, and Charleston. He bought out his partner in 1809, and made one of the great Pennsylvania fortunes prior to his death in 1847, at the age of eighty-seven. It was a dragon of his breeding that was chosen for use on the Presidential Seal.

This was the first time that the dragons of America played a major role in our history. It would be far from the last.

ABOUT THE AUTHOR

Mike Resnick is the author of 48 science fiction and fantasy novels, 12 collections, 175 short stories, and 2 screenplays, and he is the editor of 40 anthologies. He is the winner of four Hugos (from a near-record twenty-five nominations) and has won other major awards in the United States, France, Japan, Poland, Croatia, and Spain, and he has been nominated for awards in England and Italy. He has also written mysteries and nonfiction. In his spare time, he sleeps.

REALMS OF FANTASY

The largest magazine in the world devoted to fantasy.

ThinK of Things DARK AND Things DANGEROVS. Of MAGICAL LANDS AND MYSTERIOVS CREATVRES. Of HEROIC QVESTS. SVMMONED SPIRITS. SORCERY AND SWORDPLAY. TALISMANS AND DRAGONS...

FREE TRIAL ISSVE

CALL 1-800-219-1187 TO RECEIVE YOUR FREE ISSUE
Or use the coupon below to order by mail

Please send me a FREE TRIAL ISSUE of Realms of Fantasy magazine. If I like it I will receive 5 more issues. If I choose not to subscribe, I will return the bill marked "cancel" and keep the FREE trial issue. Otherwise I'll return the invoice with payment of $16.95 ($21.95 international).

AD0305

Name_____

Address_____

City_____ State_____ Zip_____

Mail To: Sovereign Media 30 W. Third Street, Third Floor, Williamsport, PA 17701

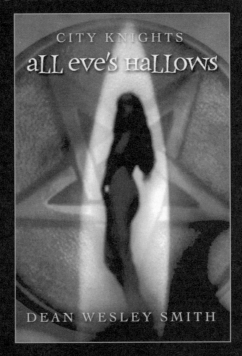

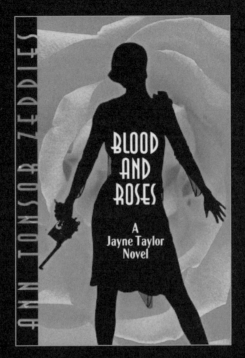

ALSO FROM PHOBOS BOOKS . . .

Empire of Dreams and Miracles
Edited by Orson Scott Card
and Keith Olexa
ISBN: 0-9720026-0-X
"...every story in Empire of Dreams
and Miracles *is a masterpiece!"*
—*Alex Black*

Hitting the Skids in Pixeltown
Edited by Orson Scott Card
and Keith Olexa
ISBN: 0-9720026-0-X
"Mind-expanding quality stories.
Hitting The Skids In Pixeltown *is
enthusiastically recommended to
every dedicated fan of science fiction."*
—*Midwest Book Review*

All the Rage This Year
Edited by Keith Olexa
ISBN: 0-9720026-5-0
*"All the Rage This Year is an excellent
anthology of stories that will surprise,
and possibly even shock, readers."*
—*Book Nook*

Absolutely Brilliant in Chrome
Edited by Keith Olexa
ISBN: 0-9720026-3-4
*"Each story is a gem, perfect, polished,
illuminating."*
—*Wigglefish.com*

Nobody Gets the Girl
James Maxey
ISBN: 0-9720026-2-6
*"[A] clever book — the pace never flags . . .
it's hard to put the book down."*
— *The SF Site*

Counterfeit Kings
Adam Connell
ISBN: 0-9720026-4-2
*"Struggle for identity and self-sacrifice
are just a few of the powerful stories beneath
an action-packed surface plot that provokes
as it dazzles." —Publishers Weekly*

PHOBOS IMPACT . . . IMPACTING THE IMAGINATION

PHOBOS IMPACT
*An Imprint of Phobos Books LLC, 200 Park Ave South, New York, NY 10003
Voice: 347-683-8151 Fax: 718-228-3597
Distributed to the trade by National Book Network 1-800-462-6420*

PHOBOS IMPACT

An Imprint of Phobos Books LLC, 200 Park Ave South, New York, NY 10003
Voice: 347-683-8151 Fax: 718-228-3597
Distributed to the trade by National Book Network 1-800-462-6420

**PHOBOS
IMPACT**

Sandra Schulberg
Publisher

John J. Ordover
Editor-in-Chief

Kathleen David
Associate Editor

Matt Galemmo
Art Director

Terry McGarry
Production Editor

Julie Kirsch
Production Coordinator

Andy Heidel
Marketing Director

Keith Olexa
Webmaster

Chris Erkmann
Advertising Associate